ЧтениЯReadings

Chtenia: Readings from Russia

a themed journal
of fiction, non-fiction, poetry,
photography and miscellany

ISSN 1939-7240 • Volume 8, Number 4 • Issue 32

Chtenia is a quarterly journal of readings from Russia, including fiction, non-fiction, memoirs, humor, poetry and photography. Opinions expressed are those of the authors and do not necessarily reflect the views of the staff, management or publisher of *Chtenia*.

Publisher: Paul E. Richardson
Managing Editor: Olga Kuzmina
Curator: José Vergara
Cover: Ilya Repin's portrait of the composer Anton Rubinstein

Chtenia Subscription rates (1 year): US $40, Outside US $50. All prices are in U.S. dollars. Back issues: when available: $10-12 (does not include shipping and handling). Newsstand: $12 per issue. • To notify us of a change of address, see the subscription address below. To ensure that you do not miss any issues, please notify us 4-6 weeks in advance of any move or address change. Periodical postage paid at Montpelier, VT and at additional mailing offices (USPS 024-769).

Publications Mail Agreement No. 40649170. Return undeliverable Canadian Address to: Station A, PO Box 54, Windsor, ON N9A 6J5. Email: orders@russianlife.com

POSTMASTER: Please send change of address and subscription applications to:
RIS Publications, PO Box 567, Montpelier, VT 05601-0567
orders@russianlife.com • ph. 802-223-4955 • www.chtenia.com

32

Musical Writing

ЧтениЯReadings
Vol. 8, No. 4 • Fall 2015 • Issue 32

Writing About Music
José Vergara

> "The significance of the tolling of church bells is preserved in the music of Mozart and Haydn. It's true that with them it becomes the tolling of love and spring. When such music reaches us on the radio, you somehow can't admit with your mind that its composer could have died."
>
> – Abram Tertz, *A Voice from the Chorus*

> "Writing about music is like dancing about architecture."
>
> – Elvis Costello

Any author who chooses to write about music faces an immense task. The most abstract of all arts, music forces the writer to put into words and descriptions – much more concrete things by comparison – its ephemeral nature. Writing about music is indeed a form of translation: it comes with its sacrifices, but it also opens up new perspectives that would otherwise remain undiscovered.

The fragile interaction between word and sound has inspired countless writers and poets in Russia. As Andrew Wachtel notes, "though literature and music may have occupied separate spheres in the Russian cultural imagination, there was constant and extremely productive interaction between them."[1] Such an exchange has gone both ways with composers (Glinka, Prokofiev, and Shostakovich to name only a few) adapting literary works for their compositions and writers taking up the subject of music in their texts.

This issue of *Chtenia* showcases a few ways in which writers have treated music. These approaches may be divided into three primary categories: texts that employ music as a structural device; works that focus on the enigmatic figure of the musician; and texts that thematically combine music with issues of memory.

Both Andrei Bely's *The Dramatic Symphony* and Abram Tertz's *The Trial Begins* show how writers have managed to transform a musical form into a literary object.Bely aimed to construct a text made up of many leitmotifs (what he called "musical phrases") that would coalesce into a unified whole and left it to the reader to notice the patterns that result. For example[2] :

5. All were pale and over everyone hung the light-blue vault of the sky, now deep-blue, now grey, now black, full of musical tedium, eternal tedium, with the sun's eye in its midst.
6. Streams of white-hot metal poured down from the same spot.
7. None knew where they ran to or why, fearing to look truth in the eye.

Schopenhauer and Nietzsche's ideas inspired Bely as he sought a means to depict the transcendental via musical principles. The opening chapter from Tertz's *The Trial Begins* adopts a related method but addresses decidedly more grounded topics. Here, a series of conversations bleed into one another as if they were parts of an overture introducing various voices that

1. Andrew Baruch Wachtel, "Introduction," *Intersections and Transpositions: Russian Music, Literature, and Society* (Evanston, IL: Northwestern University Press, 1998) xii.

2. Abram Tertz, *The Trial Begins*. Trans. Max Hayward. New York: Pantheon Books, 1960.

will be heard throughout the novella. At the chapter's bold conclusion, the musical structure resolves with a masterful description of a concert and the ways various characters respond to it.

> The music flowed. It oozed like oily, rainbow-patterned puddles. It rose. It roared and stormed off the stage into the body of the hall. Seryozha thought about the cloudburst in the streets outside and wriggled with pleasure. The music reproduced his private image of the Revolution. The flood drowned the whole of the bourgeoisie in a most convincing way.
>
> A general's wife in evening dress floundered, tried to scramble up a pillar, and was washed away. The old general swam with a vigorous breast stroke but soon sank. Even the musicians were, by now, up to their necks in water. Eyes bulging, lips spitting foam, they fiddled frenziedly, at random, below the surface of the waves....
>
> "What music!" exclaimed Globov. "That's not Prokofiev or Khachaturian for you. That's real classical stuff."
>
> He too was fascinated by the flood but he under¬stood it better than Seryozha. What struck him was that the flowing music wasn't left to its own devices, it was controlled by the conductor.[3]

Many Russian writers, including several featured here, have demonstrated a fascination with the composer/musician figure as a creative genius who rewrites rules and exudes innovation. This is the case in Nina Berberova's "The Resurrection of Mozart," Vladimir Odoyevsky's "Beethoven's Last Quartet," and Nikolai Zabolotsky's "Beethoven." These writers marvel at the composers' abilities and immortal stature. Boris Pasternak likewise describes his transformative relationship with Scriabin in his autobiography. However, not all "portraits of the musician" are quite so rosy:

....

3. Andrei Bely. *The Dramatic Symphony and the Forms of Art.* Trans. John Elsworth. Edinburgh: Polygon, 1986.

Ivan Turgenev's "The Singers" challenges the romanticized view with its titular figures who drink just as well as they sing.[4]

A number of the other chosen texts illustrate how Russian writers have traditionally viewed music as a potent mnemonic bridge or vessel. Even the notoriously tone-deaf Vladimir Nabokov, who once said he would include "no music" in his ideal state,[5] could not help but produce one of the most evocative portrayals of the ability of music to transport an individual to a past moment in his "Music." Meanwhile, Isaac Babel's "The Song" depicts the calming energy that a simple folk song has on the narrator, even as it is contrasted against the brutality of war in a jarring narrative move. Victor Pelevin's "The Tambourine of the Upper World" takes this trope in a bizarre direction, where music serves as a link between worlds.

The poems by Alexander Pushkin and Afanasy Fet exhibit on a personal level what the stories by Berberova and Odoyevsky do on a much broader one. Music in all these cases embodies a special sort of memory that, for better or worse, transcends space and time and separates the listener from his surroundings in a flash of recollection. Thanks to its very immediacy and rebelliousness, to use Nikolai Gogol's description, music penetrates both mind and emotion with ease in ways that other arts cannot. It's no wonder, then, that writers have sought to adapt it into their own art as well.

4. Not included in this issue. See: Ivan Turgenev, "The Singers," in *A Sportsmen's Notebook*, Trans. Charles and Natasha Hepburn (New York: Ecco Press, 1986) 230-248.

5. Vladimir Nabokov, *Strong Opinions* (New York: Vintage International, 1990) 34-5.

Contributors

ISAAC BABEL (1894-1940) was a journalist, playwright, translator and short story writer whose works include the masterpieces *Red Cavalry* and *The Odessa Tales*. He was loyal to the communist party but did not restrain from criticizing it. As a result of his long-term affair with the wife of NKVD chief Nikolai Yezhov, Babel was arrested in 1939 and executed in a Soviet prison in 1940, after confessing falsely to being a foreign spy and Trotskyite.

KONSTANTIN BALMONT (1867-1942) was a prolific poet and translator of Russia's Silver Age of poetry. Born into a noble family and raised with a love for languages, literature and theater, he had his first poems published at the age of 18. A leading light of the Symbolist movement, he was a tempestuous soul who was repeatedly at odds with the government, first of Tsar Nicholas, then of the Soviets. He and his family left Soviet Russia in 1920, and he lived the remainder of his life in France.

NINA BERBEROVA (1901-1993) was a writer and memoirist, and the wife of the influential metaphysical poet Vladislav Khodasevich. She gained fame for her stories about the life of émigrés in the Boulogne-Billancourt suburb of Paris but remained little-known outside the Russian émigré community. In 1985 her work was rediscovered and her novels, stories, and memoirs were translated and published to great international acclaim.

LAURENCE BOGOSLAW earned his Ph.D. in Slavic Languages from the University of Michigan in 1995. He has taught Russian language, literature, and translation courses at Gustavus Adolphus College, Macalester College,

Hamline University, the University of Minnesota, and Century College. He directs the Minnesota Translation Laboratory, a translation and consulting service that he co-founded in 1996.

ANDREW BROMFIELD is a widely published translator of Russian fiction. He is a founding editor of the Russian literature journal *Glas*, and has translated into English works by Boris Akunin, Vladimir Voinovich, Mikhail Bulgakov, Irina Denezhkina, Victor Pelevin, and Sergei Lukyanenko (including the *Night Watch* series), among other writers.

ANTON CHEKHOV (1860-1904) was a doctor, a playwright and a prolific master of the short story (having written over 400 by the time he was 26). His stories are often ironic observations on human nature that seem simple on the surface, yet hide deep veins of human emotion.

PETER CONSTANTINE is a prolific translator from several languages into English. He was awarded the National Translation Award for *The Undiscovered Chekhov: Thirty-Eight New Stories*. His translation of the complete works of Isaac Babel received the Koret Jewish Literature Award and a National Jewish Book Award citation. He has also translated Gogol's *Taras Bulba* and Tolstoy's *The Cossacks*. He is a senior editor at *Conjunctions*.

BORIS DRALYUK holds a Ph.D. in Slavic Languages and Literatures from University of California, Los Angeles. His work has appeared in a variety of journals, including *The New Yorker*, *The Times Literary Supplement*, and *World Literature Today*. He has translated and co-translated several volumes of poetry and prose from Russian and Polish and is co-editor, with Robert Chandler and Irina Mashinski, of the *Penguin Book of Russian Poetry*. His translation of Isaac Babel's *Red Cavalry* was published by Pushkin Press. He received first prize in the 2011 Compass Translation Award competition and, with Irina Mashinski, first prize in the 2012 Joseph Brodsky / Stephen Spender Translation Prize competition.

AFANASY FET (1820-1892) was one of the finest Russian poets of the nineteenth century, famous, above all, for his wonderful evocations of the world's natural beauty, but also for his poetic landscapes and love poems. He was criticized by his contemporaries for his poetry's lack of political content, the very thing that made him especially dear to many poets and writers of the Silver Age and later.

NIKOLAI GOGOL (1809-1852), in his many literary works, combined whimsically fantastic images from Ukrainian folklore with his own mystical theories. He sought to describe the multifaceted nature of Russian life, with all its absurdities, while hoping that his works would awaken the morality of his readers.

DEBORAH HOFFMAN is an attorney and freelance translator. She was the recipient of a 2005 PEN Translation Fund Grant for her translations from *Deti Gulaga*, which were recently published by Slavica under the title *The Littlest Enemies*. Her translations have appeared in the *Toronto Slavic Quarterly*, *The Literary Review*, and *Words Without Borders*. She was a Fellow for the American Literary Translators Association Conference and a recipient of a National Endowment for the Arts Translation Fellowship. She lives in Ohio.

OLGA KOSHANSKY-OLEINIKOV was a professor of Russian at the University of Illinois, Urbana.

VLADIMIR KOVNER is an engineer, a journalist, and an English-Russian translator and editor, specializing in poetry, bard songs, ballet and idioms. He and Lydia Stone have been collaborating since 2005. Vladimir was an active participant in the bard movement and his article "The Golden Age of 'Magnitizdat'" is a classic discussion of this era in Soviet history. He has contributed numerous articles to collections about Bulat Okudzhava, in addition to writing on other literary topics for books and journals in both Russian and English. He has also published two books of poetic translation, *Pet the Lion*, 2010, and *Edward Lear. The Complete Limericks with Drawings, a Bilingual English-Russian Book* (2015). He and Stone are completing work on an English-Russian idiom dictionary.

RALPH MATLAW (1927-1990) edited many translations of Russian classics and taught at Harvard, Princeton, the University of Illinois, Urbana and at the University of Chicago.

VLADIMIR NABOKOV (1899-1977) is perhaps the best-known Russian-American author. His father was a member of the 1917 Provisional Government, which forced the family to flee to Crimea and then to Western Europe. Most famous for his novel *Lolita*, Nabokov penned multiple highly acclaimed novels in English and in Russian, and went on to teach Russian poetry and literature in the United States. Early in his career he wrote under the pseudonym Vladimir Sirin.

VLADIMIR ODOYEVSKY (1803-1869) was a prominent philospher, writer, teacher, critic and philanthropist. He is best known today for his authorship of *The Russian Nights* (1844), a collection of writings that interlaced stories and novellas with philosophical conversations, yet he was also a renowned music critic.

BULAT OKUDZHAVA (1924-1997) was Georgian by nationality, but was born in Moscow and lived there nearly his entire life. A prolific composer of "author's songs" (*avtorskiye pesni*), his works were romantic and melodic, yet not overtly political. Still, his independent streak kept him from attaining official state sanction for much of his career and lead to his immense popularity among the Soviet intelligentsia, who widely distributed his recordings in *magnitizdat* form.

BORIS PASTERNAK (1890-1960) was one the greatest Russian writers of the 20th century. He was the author of many collections of poetry that exerted great influence on the development of Russian poetry. He was awarded the Nobel Prize in Literature in 1958 for his novel, *Doctor Zhivago,* but was pressured and persecuted into refusing it. Pasternak was also one of the greatest translators of the Soviet era, translating a wealth of classical texts, including Shakespeare, Goethe and others, as well as a significant number of poems.

PIERRE STEPHEN ROBERT PAYNE (1911-1983) was an extraordinarily prolific writer, historian, biographer and translator. He translated from Chinese, Danish, French, Greek, Italian, German, Polish, Spanish, and Russian. His first translation (pseudonymously as Anthony Wolfe) was Yuri Olesha's *Envy*, in 1936. Also in 1936, he became the first person to translate Pasternak's short stories into English. The result was first published in Singapore in 1941 as *Childhood*. Payne turned out an average of two books a year, many of them massive studies.

VICTOR PELEVIN studied at Moscow's Gorky Institute of Literature, and is one of the few novelists today who writes seriously about what is happening in contemporary Russia. His work has been translated into fifteen languages and his novels *Omon Ra, The Life of Insects, The Clay Machine-Gun* and *Babylon,* as well as two collections of short stories, have been published in English to great acclaim.

14

BORIS POPLAVSKY (1903-1935) was an émigré Russian poet. Both of his parents gave up music to support the family by going into business. The family fled Russia in 1919 for Ukraine (where Poplavsky read his first poetry) then moved on to Constantinople and Paris, where Poplavsky was very active in émigré culture while also continuing his education. He died of a drug poisoning along with an acquaintance, S. Yarkho, which has been variously called suicide and murder at the hands of the suicidal Yarkho, who wanted someone to accompany him to the other side.

ALEXANDER PUSHKIN (1799-1837) is considered by most to be Russia's greatest poet, which has led many to consider him the father of modern Russian literature. His life was cut short by a duel, yet he was nevertheless astoundingly prolific, and his poems are as rich and complex as they are beautiful. In his poetry and his prose, he revolutionized Russian literature by mixing storytelling and satire with vernacular language.

LYDIA RAZRAN STONE is a technical and literary translator who is the editor of *SlavFile,* the publication of the Slavic Language Division of the American Translators Association. She has been translating poetry for *Chtenia* since its first issue and curated the bilingual *Chtenia* issues devoted to Tolstoy (#20) and Okudzhava (#31). She has published four bilingual books of translated poetry, of which the two most recent, *The Frogs Who Begged for a Tsar (and 61 other Russian fables by Ivan Krylov)*, and *The Little Humpbacked Horse* were published by Russian Life Books.

MARIAN SCHWARTZ is a prize-winning translator of Russian fiction, history, biography, criticism, and fine art. She has translated authors as diverse as Slavnikova, Lermontov and Goncharov, and is the principal English translator of the works of Nina Berberova. Her most recent translations include Mikhail Shishkin's *Maidenhair* and Andrei Gelasimov's *The Lying Year.* Schwartz is the recipient of two translation fellowships from the National Endowment for the Arts and is a past president of the American Literary Translators Association.

BORIS SLUTSKY (1919-1986) was a Ukrainian born poet who wrote in Russian. His experiences in World War II had a great impact on his coarse and conversational poetry, and he was one of the most important representatives of the "war generation" of Russian poets. Soon after Stalin's death, verses that some attributed to Slutsky, and that were highly critical of

Stalinism, circulated in *samizdat*. Slutsky never confirmed or denied his authorship.

JOSÉ VERGARA is a Ph.D. candidate in the Department of Slavic Languages and Literature at the University of Wisconsin-Madison. His current research focuses on the intertextual relations between James Joyce and Russian writers such as Vladimir Nabokov and Andrei Bitov. He has published articles on Yury Olesha and the Czech multilingual poet Ivan Blatný, as well as a book chapter on Daniil Kharms.

NIKOLAI ZABOLOTSKY (1903-1958) was a distinguished poet and translator. In his youth, he penned absurdist poetry and was a member of the OBERIU society, a collective of Russian futurist writers. However, over time, influenced by both internal and external forces, Zabolotsky began to compose more realistic poetry. In 1938 he was arrested, and from 1943 he lived in internal exile. Zabolotsky was not allowed to moved to Moscow and lived for many years in the Caucasus, primarily in Georgia, where he developed close ties through friendship and literature. There, in addition to writing poetry, he masterfully translated Georgian works into Russian.

Posthumous portrait of Wolfgang Amadeus Mozart
Barbara Kraft (1819)

The Resurrection of Mozart
Nina Berberova

I

In the early days of June 1940, just at the time when the French army was beginning its final and irrevocable retreat after the breach at Sedan, on a quiet warm evening, a group of four women and five men were sitting in a garden under the trees, about thirty miles from Paris. They were in fact talking about Sedan, talking of how the last few days had restored to that name which, like crinoline, had long since gone out of fashion, the ominous connotations it had had before; this town, which none of them had ever seen, and which had died in the time of their grandfathers, seemed to have been resurrected in order to relive the tragic events that were destined for it alone.

The silence was so complete that when they stopped talking and returned to their own private thoughts, they could hear through the open windows the clock ticking in the large old house. The sky was green, clear, and lovely, and the stars were just beginning to shine, so few and far-flung that they failed to form any definite pattern. The old trees – acacias, limes – neither breathed nor trembled, as if standing stock-still were a safeguard against something that was invisible to men but somehow immanent in the summer evening. The hosts and their guests had just finished supper; the table had not yet been cleared. Some wineglasses were still on the table. Slowly, the green light of the darkening sky transformed the faces of the seated company, which were now obscured by shadows. They were talking about war and about the omens of war. A young woman, a guest who had driven out from town with her husband and sister, restraining her brassy voice, remarked that she had seen a meteor a fortnight before.

"It was about this time of day. The sky was just as hazy. At first it looked like a falling star, but it was so long and it was so bright."

"You probably wouldn't even have noticed it a year ago," said another guest, smiling. This was Chabarov, a bald, robust man with a drooping black mustache and wearing a bright blue shirt. He was a groundsman at a chateau about eight miles away and had just arrived on his bicycle.

"A year ago," said Vassily Georgievich Sushkov, the host, a tall man, taller than anyone else at the table, gray-haired but not yet old, with a sharp and furtive look in his eye. "Yes, it was exactly a year ago today that Nevelsky died. He knew a lot of this was coming. He predicted so much of it."

"Well, he couldn't have picked a better time to die. At least he doesn't have to see what we see. If he were resurrected he'd either spit in disgust or break down and cry."

Facing the hostess, at the opposite end of the table, sat a Frenchman brought along by Chabarov but whom no one else really knew. Simply, and without any fussy apology, he asked them to translate what they were all saying.

"Monsieur Daunou, we were talking about the dead, and what they would say if they were resurrected and saw what's going on now," replied Maria Leonidovna Sushkova.

Daunou took his black pipe out of his mouth, furrowed his brow, and smiled.

"Is it worth waking the dead?" he said, looking his hostess straight in the eye. "I suppose I might well invite Napoleon to come and have a look at our times, but I'd certainly spare my parents the pleasure."

Suddenly everyone started talking at once.

"Resurrect them for your sake or for theirs? I don't understand," Manyura Krein, who had come from Paris, asked with a lively expression, not addressing anyone in particular and no longer trying to conceal her loud voice. She had a full mouth of her very own white teeth, which gave the impression of being false. "If it were for their sake, then of course you'd resurrect Napoleon and Bismarck and Queen Victoria, and maybe even Julius Caesar. But if I could bring someone from the past back to life for my sake, just for mine, then that's an entirely different thing. That calls for some thought. Such a large choice, so many temptations... still, silly as it sounds, I think I'd resurrect Pushkin."

"A charming, fun-loving, marvelous man," said Maria Leonidovna Sushkova. "What a joy it would be to see him alive."

"Or maybe Taglioni?" continued Manyura Krein.

"I'd lock her up at home so I could look at her whenever I wanted."

"And then take her to America," put in Chabarov, "and let the impresarios tear her to shreds."

"Come on, if you're going to resurrect anyone, then don't resurrect Taglioni," said Fyodor Egorovich Krein with barely repressed irritation. He was Manyura's husband, twice her age, and a friend of Sushkov's. "There's no need to be frivolous. I would make the best of the occasion. I would drag Tolstoy back into God's world. Wasn't it you, dear sir, who denied the role of the individual in history? You who declared that there would be no more wars? And wasn't it you who took a skeptical view of vaccination? No, don't try to wriggle out of it now. Just have a look at the result." It was evident that Fyodor Egorovich had scores to settle with Tolstoy and that he had an entire text prepared should they happen to meet in the next life.

"*Avec Taglioni on pourrait faire fortune,*" Chabarov repeated his thought in French.

"And I, gentlemen," piped in Sushkov's mother, who wore heavy violet powder and reeked of some unpleasant perfume, "and I, gentlemen, would resurrect Uncle Lyosha. Wouldn't he be surprised?"

No one knew who Uncle Lyosha was, so no one said anything for a minute or two. Little by little the conversation had drawn everyone in, taking them far from that evening, that garden, and into the past, the recent or the very distant past, as if someone had already made a firm promise to wave a magic wand and fulfill everyone's wish, so that now the only problem was in making a choice, and it was a difficult choice because no one wanted to miscalculate, especially the women.

"No one but Mozart will do for me, though. Yes, it has to be Mozart," Maria Leonidovna thought. "There's no one else I want, and it would be useless anyway."

She had decided not out of any morbid love of music, as can happen with women who have reached a certain age and who are generally thought of as "cultured," but merely because she connected that name in her mind with her earliest childhood, and because it lived on as something pure, transparent, and eternal that might take the place of happiness. Maria Leonidovna smoked avidly and waited for someone else to say something. She didn't feel like talking herself. It was Magdalena, Manyura Krein's sister, a young woman of thirty, full-figured and pale, with unusually rounded shoulders, who spoke up. The sight of her always brought to mind those undeniable statistics about how in Europe so many millions of young women had been left single because there weren't enough husbands to go round.

"No, I wouldn't resurrect a single famous man," said Magdalena, with a certain disdain for men of renown. "I'd much prefer an ordinary mortal. An idealistic youth from the early nineteenth century, a follower of Hegel, a reader of Schiller; or a courtier to one of the French kings."

She shrugged her heavy shoulders and looked around. But already it was nearly dark, and one could barely make out the faces round the table. But the stars were now quite visible overhead, and the sky seemed familiar again.

Chabarov didn't say anything for a long while. Finally he made a muffled nasal sound, drummed his fingers on the table, opened his mouth, but suddenly hesitated, said nothing, and sank back into his thoughts.

The ninth person present, who had been silent until then, was Kiryusha, Sushkov's nineteen-year-old son and Maria Leonidovna's stepson. In the family he was considered a little backward. Slowly he unglued his thick, wide lips and, gazing trustfully at his stepmother with his blue and very round eyes, asked if it was possible to resurrect two people at the same time.

God alone knows what was going through his dreamy mind at that point. He seemed to think that everything had already been decided by the others and that only the details remained to be settled.

"Mais c'est un vrai petit jeu," noted Daunou with a sad laugh, and immediately everyone seemed to move and smile once more, as if returning from far away. "Everyone has their own private passion, and everyone is being terribly serious about it."

Maria Leonidovna just nodded at him. "Mozart, of course, only Mozart will do," she repeated to herself. "And it's a good thing I'm not young anymore and don't have any physical interest in seeing him. We could sit up till dawn, and he could play our piano and we'd talk. And everyone would come to see him and listen to him – the neighbors' gardener and his wife, the postman, the shopkeeper and his family, the stationmaster... What a joy it would be! And tomorrow there'd be no post, no trains, nothing at all. Everything would be topsy-turvy. And there wouldn't be any war. No, there would be war all the same."

She lit another cigarette. For a moment the match illuminated her thin, slightly worn face and her delicate, beautiful hands. Everything about her, except her face, was feminine, youthful, and sleek, particularly her light and silent walk. Everyone noticed when Maria Leonidovna suddenly got up and walked out under the trees, and then came back to the table, and they could see the lit end of her cigarette in the darkness of the advancing night.

A chill came up about then from the low-lying part of the garden, where two little stone bridges crossed the narrow loops of the flower-banked stream. Old Mrs. Sushkova, wrapped in a shawl, was dozing in her chair. Kiryusha was looking up blankly, and it was clear that like the trees and stars he was merely existing and not thinking. And suddenly, somewhere far off, perhaps twenty-five or thirty miles away to the east, where the sun rises in the summer, the sound of gunfire rumbled, burst out, and then disappeared. It was very much like thunder and yet completely different.

"Time we were on our way," everyone started saying immediately, and Manyura Krein, jangling her bracelets, ran into the house for her coat and bag.

They went through the dining room and big dark hallway and came out into the yard where the car was parked. Sushkov's mother was going back to Paris as well. She put on a hat with a big violet-colored flower; even her suitcase was a shade of violet. The motor idled a few moments, and then, cautiously spreading its black wings, the car backed up to the gates. Krein, sitting behind the steering wheel, waved once again to those left behind. Manyura, whose porcelain mouth alone was illuminated, smiled behind the glass and said something. The car started up, stopped, shifted into forward, and, as if it had hauled itself out, disappeared, leaving behind it a wake of invisible, acrid exhaust.

Chabarov went to find the bicycles.

"We'd be very happy to see you here any time," Sushkov told the Frenchman. "We're staying all summer, and on Sundays, as you see, our friends visit. You're always welcome."

"*Enchanté, monsieur,*" Daunou replied. "I have spent an unforgettable evening."

And following behind Chabarov he kissed Maria Leonidovna's hand.

The next day, as usual, Vassily Georgievich took the train into town, leaving Maria Leonidovna and Kiryusha to themselves. That Monday, at one o'clock in the afternoon, several dozen airplanes bombed Paris for the first time.

News of the bombardment of Paris only came that evening. During the day you could hear the gunfire, but it was so far away that you couldn't tell whether it was in Paris or Pontoise, where it had been a few days before. In the evening the papers arrived, and all the people who lived in the little village, in the center of which stood a neglected church with a caved-in roof, came spilling out into the modest avenue of sturdy plane trees that led from the cafe to the *mairie*.

The village consisted almost entirely of old women. Of course they might have only been, as in any French village, about half the population, but they were the ones you saw most often. Seeing them out in the street, talking together or shopping or shaking out a rug or hanging out clothes, they seemed to make up nine-tenths of the inhabitants.

Some of them were no more than fifty, and they were still smart and cheerful, just turning gray, rosy-cheeked and sharp-eyed. Others were wrinkled and toothless, with swollen veins. Others, who could remember the invasion of the Germans in 1870, were hunched up and barely able to put one sore foot in front of the other, and they had darkened hands, long black nails, and lifeless faces. They were all much of a kind, talking to each other in the same way, and using the same words, wherever they met, be it on street corners, beneath the plane trees, or by their front gates. They all wore wide calico aprons that either tied at the back or buttoned in front. Some wore steel glasses on their noses and knitted, rocking in a chair and holding the skein of wool under their left arms. Almost all of them were widows of men killed in the last war, and all without exception had seen either a son or a son-in-law set off for this war.

That evening, in the shady lane that ran alongside the fence to the Sushkovs' garden, the silence was broken. Kiryusha came to tell Maria Leonidovna that Paris had been bombed, buildings destroyed, warehouses burned, and more than a thousand killed or wounded. Maria Leonidovna looked at Kiryusha, who was smiling broadly, and it saddened her that this human being, who was now completely grown, was still the same child she had first met twelve years before. There was a time – and lately she had thought of it often – when he had suddenly decided to learn the alphabet. A brief light had pierced the darkness of that sick brain. He had tried to learn the letters, but nothing ever came of it. It had all ended with Kiryusha's short and relatively happy affair with the girl who worked in the charcuterie. Relatively happy because after that he had started to get gradually worse.

Maria Leonidovna went through Paris in her mind. In that city, above all, was Vassily Georgievich, as well as their pretty, sunny, quiet apartment, which she loved so much. Then there were the Kreins, the Abramovs, the Snezhinskys, Edouard Zontag, Semyon Isaakovich Freiberg, Lenochka Mikhailova, and many many more who could have been wounded or killed. And when she thought about all those people living at various ends of the city, scattered across the old creased map of Paris that she kept in her mind, a flashing light lit up, here and there, and then went out.

"Yes. This had to happen," she told herself. "We were talking about it only yesterday. So why did he go? The Kreins could have stayed on, too. Yesterday we said... What else were we talking about yesterday? Oh, yes! 'You are God, Mozart, and of that fact yourself innocent. One ought to aspire to something that combines everything beautiful, pure and eternal, like those clouds, not all these terrible things, all these murders and lies. Before the ultimate silence closes in on you, shouldn't you listen to what the stars are saying to each other?"

She went over to the little radio, brand-new, which Kiryusha was strictly forbidden to go near, and turned the knob. First a French voice spoke, then an English voice, then a German voice. All of it was crammed into that wooden box, separated only by invisible barriers. The voices all said the same thing. And suddenly it switched to music, singing, Spanish or maybe Italian, the voluptuous and carefree strumming of a guitar. But she picked up the word *amore,* and she turned the machine off and walked to the window, from which she could see the village road among the thick fields of oats, green and ash gray.

On Tuesday, Wednesday, and Thursday, soldiers were billeted in the village: heavy green trucks camouflaged with foliage as if decked out for a carnival and bearing numbers written in red lead paint brought in five hundred young, healthy, raucous soldiers and four officers wearing long overcoats and with tired, worried, feverish faces. A billeting officer appeared at Maria Leonidovna's door – the house the Sushkovs rented was by far the best in the village – and she immediately moved Kiryusha into the dining room, giving his room to the captain and the space in the annex to three sublieutenants.

The four officers slept in their clothes. The sentry – sometimes a short, swarthy, and yellow-eyed man or else a tall, erect, and big-faced one – came to wake them several times during the night. Vassily Georgievich called every day; his call came to the post office at the corner of their side street and the square. A little boy missing his front teeth ran to fetch Maria Leonidovna, and she ran after him in her silent, girlish way, wearing whatever she happened to have on, ran into the tiny single-windowed building, picked up the receiver, and listened to Vassily Georgievich say that everything was fine, that he had received the money, seen Edouard, was eating with the Snezhinskys, would arrive on Saturday.

"I have soldiers staying with me," she said, still out of breath from running. "I've given them Kiryusha's room. And the annex."

"Maybe I should come? You're not afraid?"

"Why should I be afraid? Good-bye." And in fact, at that minute, she thought that she wasn't afraid in the least. In a way, it was even reassuring to have these polite, laconic men close at hand.

But at night she barely slept. She listened. From far away, in the dead of night, she caught the diffuse, persistent sound of a motorcycle. While the sound was on the far side of the woods, it was no more than a whisper, but as it got nearer it became louder and more focused, and then suddenly it was zooming down the lane and stopping at the house next door, where the sentry was posted. The motor was switched off, and then she could hear voices, steps. The gate banged. Someone was walking into the house, into her house, some stranger, and the old blind dog got up from its straw and went to sniff at his tracks in the gravel of the yard, growling. A light went on somewhere, she heard someone running through the house, through the annex. Something clinked, a door slammed. Kiryusha was asleep close by, in the dining room, whose door she left open. These night sounds didn't frighten her anymore. What frightened her was everything that was going on in the world that night.

She wasn't afraid of the quiet strangers either. They left the third night, leaving the doors and the gate wide open, leaving the village in trucks camouflaged with fresh branches. She wasn't afraid of the sentries who came to see them or of the five hundred strong, half-sober soldiers quartered all over the village. She was afraid of the air, the warm June air, through which gunfire rolled across the horizon and submerged her, her house, and her garden, along with the summer clouds. And there was no question that this puff of wind, which was somehow just like time itself, would in the end bring something terrible and ruinous, such as death itself. Just as, looking at the calendar, no one doubted any longer that in five, ten, or fifteen days something dreadful was going to happen, so, feeling that faint breeze on her face day and night, she could say with assurance that it would bring to these parts murder, occupation, devastation, and darkness.

For the air, over the last few days, had been warm, clear, and fragrant. Kiryusha worked in the garden, watering the flowers in front of the house every evening and looking after the neighbors' ducklings. Maria Leonidovna, wearing a bright cotton print dress, and a scarf around her head, went to clean out the annex, where she found a bag of cartridges that had been left behind and two unsealed letters, which she threw away without reading. There were cigarette butts in the cup by the washstand, and a charred newspaper lay on the floor. She made up Kiryusha's bed in his room and when the woman from next door came over to do the housework, told her to wash all the floors in the house.

On the same day, toward evening, fugitives from Soissons arrived at the neighbors': two fat, pale women, an old man, and some children. A mattress was laid out on the roof of their filthy car, and to the amazed questioning of the villagers the new arrivals explained that this was what everybody was doing now, that this was what would protect you from bullets. The old man was carried into the house by his hands and feet: he was unconscious.

Before night other fugitives arrived to stay in the sky-blue, toylike house opposite the church. People said that some of the soldiers were still there, and were spending the night at the other end of the village. There seemed to be a stranger who had come from far away by foot or by car hiding in every house for the night. There were no lights, all was dark, but voices could be heard everywhere from behind the shutters; the cafe was full of shouting and singing. Under the plane trees the old ladies, who had stayed longer than was normal, spoke in low voices.

Maria Leonidovna locked the front door, hung the curtains over the windows, cleared away the remains of supper, and, as she always did, sat in the next room and talked with Kiryusha while he got ready for bed. From time to time he exclaimed happily:

"I cleaned my teeth! I took off my left shoe!"

And if you didn't know it was a nineteen-year-old man in there – who ate enormous meals, snored loudly in his sleep, and couldn't read – you would think it was a ten-year-old boy going to bed and, for a joke, talking in a bass voice.

After she had turned out the lights in the dining room and Kiryusha's room and went to her own, she stood for a long time by the open window and looked out at where, in the daytime, she could see the road and the oat fields. Tomorrow Vassily Georgievich was due to return. The idea was pleasant and consoling. But today Maria Leonidovna had barely given a thought to her husband; in fact she hadn't stopped thinking about Mozart.

Or rather, not about Mozart himself. Right now, as a new crescent moon appeared on the edge of this anxious but subdued night, her thoughts took on a special clarity. All day long, or rather, over the last few days and this evening, she had been asking herself the same question, and there was no answer to it: Why was it that horror, cruelty, and affliction made themselves felt so easily, became concrete and weighed all the more heavily, whereas everything sublime, gentle, unexpected, and full of charm cast a frail shadow across the heart and thoughts, so one couldn't touch it or look at it closely or feel its shape and weight?

"Except for love, of course," she thought, standing by the window. "Only love gives that kind of joy. But what about someone who doesn't want to love anymore, who can no longer love? I have no one to love; it's too late for me. I have a husband, I don't need anyone else."

And all of a sudden she thought she heard the latch on the gate click, and she distinctly heard someone come into the yard, take two steps, and stop.

"Who's there?" she asked quietly.

The darkness was not yet total, and the faint, blurred shadow of a man lay on the whitish gravel in the yard. The shadow moved and the gravel crunched. The man must have been able to see Maria Leonidovna clearly as she stood in the open window, to the right of the front door. The door, as Maria Leonidovna recalled, was locked. But the man, who was slowly and purposefully walking across the yard, made no response. She could hardly see him. He walked up the porch stairs, stopped three paces away from Maria Leonidovna, put out his hand, and the door opened. And when he had already walked into the house, she wanted to scream. But, as in a dream, she was unable to produce any sound.

He was pale and thin, with a long nose and tangled hair. Everything he had on, from his shoes to his hat, seemed to have been borrowed from someone else. His dusty hands were so slender and frail that he couldn't have used them even if he had wanted to. His face was weary, youthful, but it wasn't a boy's face. She could tell that he looked younger than he was, but that in fact he could be over thirty.

"Forgive me for frightening you," he said in French, but with a slight foreign accent. "Could I spend the night here somewhere?"

By the light of the lamp illuminating the spacious entryway Maria Leonidovna looked at him, standing silently and barely able to control herself. But the moment he uttered those first words and looked at her with his long, hesitant look, her fear passed, and she asked:

"Who are you?"

But he dropped his eyes.

"Where are you from?"

He shivered slightly, and his fingers clutched the upturned collar of his ample jacket, which might have been covering an otherwise naked body.

"Oh, from far, far away... and I'm so tired. I'd like to lie down somewhere, if that's all right."

"A fugitive," she decided, "and maybe he's a Frenchman from some out-of-the-way province. Judging by his age, he could be a soldier; by his clothes, a fugitive? Maybe a spy?"

She led him to the annex, thinking all the time that he might strike her from behind, but at the same time knowing he wouldn't. By the time they had entered the bedroom, she had lost all fear of him. He didn't even look around, but silently walked over to the bed, sat down on it, and closed his eyes. Between his shoe and trouser leg she saw a thin, bare ankle.

"Do you want to eat?" she asked, closing the shutters on the low, folding windows from inside. "It's the war, we're not supposed to show any light on the outside."

"What did you say?" he asked, shuddering a little.

"I asked whether you'd like to eat something."

"No, thank you. I had a bite to eat in your local restaurant. They were all full up, though, and couldn't give me a place to stay."

She realized it was time she went.

"Are you alone?" she spoke again, rearranging something on the table as she passed.

"What do you mean 'alone'?"

"I mean, did you come here – to the village – with friends or what?"

He raised his eyes.

"I came alone, just as I am, without any luggage," he said, smiling but not revealing his teeth. "And I'm not a soldier, I'm a civilian. A musician."

She took another look at his hands, said good-night, and, having shown him where to turn off the light, walked out of the room.

That time she gave two turns to the lock in the door and suddenly, feeling a strangely animal weariness, went straight to bed and fell asleep. In the morning, as always, she got up early. Kiryusha was already in the garden bawling out some song, and in the annex all was quiet.

III

Just before lunch she wondered, anxiously, if something had happened: the shutters and door were still closed. "Can he still be asleep?" she thought. At four o'clock Vassily Georgievich was due to arrive, and a little before then she went again to see whether her lodger was up. She half opened the door to the tiny entryway, and then the door of the room. The man was sleeping, breathing evenly. He had not removed any of his clothes, not even his shoes. He lay on his back on the wide mattress, the pillow on one side. Maria Leonidovna closed the door again.

Vassily Georgievich was late getting back; the train coming from Paris had stopped for a long time at some bridge. Sushkov had carried a large suitcase from the station to the house, practically a trunk, on his broad, strong shoulder. It was full of things gathered up from their Paris apartment, without which Vassily Georgievich could not imagine either his own or his wife's existence. There were his winter coat, Maria's old squirrel coat, warm underwear which he always wore during the winter, an album of photographs of Prague (he had lived in Czechoslovakia for a long time), expensive binoculars in their case, a pound of dried figs, which he liked to keep in reserve, a handsomely bound edition of Montesquieu's *Lettres Persanes*, and Maria Leonidovna's ball gown, sewn for a charity ball the year before at which she had sold champagne. Maria Leonidovna was surprised to see warm underwear and heavy coats in

June. But Sushkov assured her that they might be cut off from Paris or could be forced to escape, and then they wouldn't know what was going to happen.

"Escape from here? Yes, of course, we'll have to escape if everyone else does. Those fugitives from Soissons are packing up their things again, and the old man is being carried out of the house to the car." She took up the newspaper her husband had brought but learned nothing from it. Vassily Georgievich spoke to her sensibly and gently. Sometimes he argued with himself, sometimes he told her what Snezhinsky and Freiberg thought about what was going on. And everything he said was accurate, fair, intelligent.

"So, your officers have gone, have they?" he asked her. "It must have been worrying for you."

"They're gone, but since yesterday there's been a" – she wanted to say "fellow" but couldn't – "man sleeping, staying in the annex. He's still asleep. He must have come the seventy-five miles on foot."

"My God, you've been staying here alone with my idiot and you're not afraid to let in strangers," he exclaimed, never mincing words when it concerned Kiryusha. And catching her hand, scratching himself on her sharp nails, he kissed it several times.

Toward the end of the day Kiryusha told them in his incoherent way that the man staying in the annex had gone. An hour later Maria Leonidovna heard him return and lock himself in again.

"That man came back. He must be sleeping again. Don't you go bothering him," she told Kiryusha.

All the next day was the same: the visitor either lay or sat by the window and neither moved nor spoke. It was as if he were waiting for something. Or else he walked to the village for a little while, walked down the lane, across the square, down the avenue of plane trees, bought himself something to eat, and came back quietly.

Strange thoughts occurred to Maria Leonidovna. Sometimes she thought that the man was bound to be arrested. Why hadn't he told her his name? Why was he wearing clothes that didn't belong to him? If he wasn't a spy, then he was a deserter. Maybe he was Russian? In many years of living abroad, Maria Leonidovna had grown used to the fact that there were no half-mad Frenchmen. Did he have a passport or had he thrown everything away, lost it? Had he run out of the house in his underwear and then received clothes from good-hearted people on the way? But perhaps there was nothing wrong, and he was just a lonely musician who had been turned out from where he sawed away at his fiddle or gave lessons to young ladies or composed just for himself, dreaming of world acclaim.

But these thoughts came and went, and life went on without interruption. This Sunday was nothing at all like the last, when they had sat in the garden over the samovar with the Kreins. No one came from town. Chabarov and Daunou arrived at five o'clock on bicycles. The three men sat in Vassily Georgievich's study for a long time and talked, about the war, of course, but in a different way than they had the week before: they were talking about their hopes. Daunou talked about his own hopes, about how they could still put a stop to this insane, iron advance at the Seine and the Marne. Each time Maria Leonidovna looked in on them she had the feeling that the Frenchman wanted to tell her something. He got up and spoke to her in particular, and for some reason she found that unpleasant. He gave her the impression (only her, though) of being a hysteric, and when she left the room she was afraid of running into him later in the dining room, the yard, the garden.

She couldn't have explained her feeling, but Daunou's serious, determined, overly expressive face was before her all the time. She started to make tea, and he came out into the dining room, closing the door behind him as if in despair, and Maria Leonidovna felt that he was about to tell her something she would remember the rest of her life.

"Nous sommes perdus, madame," he said quietly, looking into her face with his small eyes of indeterminate color. "Even the Emperor Napoleon himself, whom I wanted to resurrect last Sunday, couldn't do

anything now. I'm telling only you this. You make your own decision about where and when you should leave. *Paris est sacrifié.*"[1]

He turned white. His face contorted. But he coughed awkwardly, and everything fell into place again. She was left, frozen, holding the porcelain sugar bowl.

"There will not be a battle on the Loire. The Maginot Line will be taken from the west. Nothing at all is going to happen. It's all over. They'll go all the way to Bordeaux, to the Pyrenees. And then we'll sue for peace."

At that moment Vassily Georgievich and Chabarov walked out into the dining room, and everyone sat down at the table.

She believed Daunou, but not completely, and for that reason when she and Vassily Georgievich were alone again she was unable to convince him that everything would be as Daunou had said. She said, "You know, I think it would be best if you didn't go back to Paris again. Let's pack up tomorrow and move to the South, all three of us, Tuesday at the latest. We can spend a month or two in Provence, until things calm down. Like everyone else."

He listened to her thoughtfully, but couldn't agree.

"What would they say about me at the office? They'd call me a coward. Tomorrow I'm going to Paris, and I give you my word of honor, I'll be back on Wednesday. Even if all's well, I'll be back. Haven't we seen plenty in our time? For them this is terrible, but we've seen a lot worse... 'Nothing happens at a pace like that, a pace like that,'" he sang brightly.

The next day she was left alone again with Kiryusha. The traveler was still in the annex.

He continued to get up late, sit by the window, and look out at the yard, at the trees, at the sky. Sitting erect, his hands placed on the windowsill, he looked and listened with a sad and equal attention both to the birds moving about in the lilac bushes and to the distant gunfire and the human talk beyond the gates and in the house. Once or twice he got up, put on his faded, outsize hat, or picked it up, and went out, softly shutting the gate.

---

1. "We are lost, madame...Paris has been sacrificed."

He walked through the village, taking a good look at what was going on, since every day the people got more and more worried, agitated, and grim. In the evenings he sat for a long time, no longer at the window but on the threshold to the annex, his eyes half-closed, his hand lazily resting on the head of the old dog, who came to sit next to him.

Night fell; the moon glimmered. There was something menacing about the clear sky, the quiet fields, the roads running to and fro, this summer, this world where fate had compelled him to live. When he rested his head on his hand, it seemed he was trying to remember something and that was why he was so quiet, that he couldn't do it. Where was he from? And where should he go, and did he have to go any farther? And what was life, this pulse, this breathing, this waiting, what was this ecstasy, this grief, this war? He was so weak, but he had a powerful harmony in his heart, a melody in his head. Why was he here among all this, among the now incessant noise of the gunfire, among these preparations for departure in village families, where they led out horses, tied up cows, where they sewed up gold into the lining of clothes? He had nothing. Not even a pack. No family, no lover to sew him a shirt, cook him soup, rumple and warm his bed. All he had was music. That's how he had grown up, that's how it had been since he was a child. Feet to carry him, hands to fend off people, and music, and that was it. But there was no point coming, no, no point coming into a world where he would always go unrecognized and unheard, where he was weaker than a shadow, poorer than a bird, as guileless as the simplest flower of the field. When Kiryusha saw that the dog was sitting beside him and wasn't afraid, he came and sat as well, not daring to sit on the porch, but close by, on a stone. And so all three of them sat for a long time, in silence, until it got dark, and then Kiryusha, taking a deep breath, let out a long, idiotic laugh and went into the house.

On Wednesday morning Vassily Georgievich did not come back. There had been no telephone communication with Paris for two days, and Maria Leonidovna had absolutely no idea what to think. People were saying that there weren't any trains, that the papers hadn't come out, that travel across Paris was impossible, and that people had been deserting Paris for two days. The entire village was packing up and leaving. Those who only the night before had criticized people fleeing in fear were themselves loading things onto carts, cars, and prams. A swarm of little boys and girls sped around on bicycles. Three rows of small trucks and cars filed down the main road, which passed less than a mile from the village.

During the day rumors had been flying around, the gunfire went on constantly, growing ever nearer, and silver airplanes sailed high in the sky. Several cars, trying to take a shortcut, wound up on the avenue of plane trees and couldn't figure out how to get out, so they looped back and returned to the main road, nosing into the endless chain and continuing southward.

There were artillery, gypsy caravans, trucks loaded with ledgers (and on them sat pale bookkeepers, evacuating the bank, the foundation of the state); people on foot, on bicycles, broken-rank cavalrymen on light horses interspersed with Percherons harnessed to long wagons carrying sewing machines, kitchen utensils, furniture, barrels. And high above all the goods and chattels were perched old women, deathly pale and bareheaded; some old women sat in cars, while others went on foot, alone or supported by the arm. Troops hauled decrepit cannons, and an empty van surmounted by a magnificent red cross followed behind a sports car out of which leaned a lop-eared dog that looked like a soft toy. Then came the wounded, some of them sitting despondently, holding on to their own leg or arm, a stump that dripped blood on the road. Others vomited air and saliva. People carried hay, unthreshed wheat, factory lathes, tanks of oil. And this odd stream could be seen all the way to the horizon, living and yet already dead.

Up until nightfall Maria Leonidovna cleaned and packed, fully aware that Vassily Georgievich couldn't come by train, just as they couldn't leave by train. From the house she could see the main road, and since morning she had watched the relentless, slowly flowing, sometimes pausing, river of fugitives. The thought that she might be left alone after everyone was gone worried her, and above all the thought that Vassily Georgievich might not return. She was worried as well about Kiryusha, who in the rising panic had suddenly become grotesquely incoherent. In the middle of the day she saw her silent guest a few times, and even greeted him from a distance. She resolved to have a chat with him, find out about him, maybe help him out, and that decision preoccupied her for a few minutes. The evening came, she prepared supper, and just as they were sitting down she heard the sound of a motor, a comforting, familiar sound. Two cars drove into the Sushkovs' yard: in one sat the three Kreins; in the other, Edouard Zontag, Vassily Georgievich, and old Mrs. Sushkova. Both cars had left Paris the previous evening. They had been on the road all night and all day.

Manyura Krein broke down in tears when she walked into the house. "This is too much! Simply too much!" she said with her large mouth. "This is not to be endured. Children are being led along on foot, old people are hobbling on crutches. I'll never forget this as long as I live."

But Maria Leonidovna scarcely got to hug her because she had to say hello to Zontag and to Magdalena and follow her husband into the next room and listen to his agitated story about how yesterday afternoon he had realized that she was right, that they should have left on Sunday, that now they might not make it.

"Kiryusha's not too good," she told him, since even today she considered that that was the most important thing.

Edouard Zontag had long-standing business ties with Vassily Georgievich, and relations between them, for some reason only they understood, were rather strained. He kept aloof, apparently looking on the Kreins as relatives of Maria Leonidovna, and smoked a fat cigar. He was short and used to say that the shorter the man, the fatter the cigar he smoked.

An omelette, cold meat, salad, cheese, an apple tart, just appeared on the table, all at once, and they launched into it haphazardly and greedily, letting the abundance of that house fill them with contentment, fully aware that tomorrow it would all be gone. They drank a lot and talked a lot. They discussed how and when the decision had been made to surrender Paris, the bombing of its northern and western suburbs, and especially how everyone had dropped everything and fled, not only those who had been preparing for it but also those who had had no desire whatsoever to budge; how that night, in total darkness, it took them five hours to get from their apartment to the city limits. How they had been surrounded by thousands upon thousands of others like themselves, how the engine died on them, the radiator boiled over, and they took turns sleeping.

Then they had a conference: What time tomorrow should they go and which road was best? They bent over the map for a long time, sketched something, drew it out, and then drank again and even had another bite to eat, especially the men. In the yard an old lady slaughtered two hens, and Manyura cleaned them on the big kitchen table, lowered her fingers, covered in rings, with varnished nails, down into it, and drew out something slippery.

Magdalena and Maria Leonidovna, sitting on their heels by the linen closet, looked for one more pillow case for Edouard. The men were trying to decide whether or not to drive over to pick up Chabarov, and old Mrs. Sushkova wanted to express her opinion too, but no one was listening to her.

She went to her room, that is, to Kiryusha's room, where she was supposed to spend the night, and it immediately began to reek of her perfume in there. Room was found for the Kreins in the house, but Edouard Zontag had to be put in the annex.

"Wait for me, I'll be back in a minute," said Maria Leonidovna, and she ran across the yard.

She knocked on the door. He was lying on the bed but not sleeping, and when she came in he raised himself and slowly lowered his long legs in their torn shoes and ran his hand over his hair, as if he wanted to smooth it, comb it, give it some semblance of order. She started speaking softly, scarcely glancing in his direction.

"Excuse me, but something's come up. We have a full house. People didn't sleep last night, and there's nowhere to put them. Please, we have a small shed by the garage. Move over there. I feel bad disturbing you, but you understand, there's nothing else I can do. And then, in any case, we'll be leaving early tomorrow morning and you'll have to leave too because we'll be locking up and taking the keys with us. You won't be able to stay."

He stood up and in the semi-dark (a cold bleak light fell from the entry-way where a small lamp was lit) started pacing around the room, evidently at a loss how best to answer her.

"Tomorrow morning? Then why move to the shed? I'll leave tonight."

She couldn't help feeling glad that he'd said this.

"I feel that I'm chasing you away, practically in the middle of the night. Please stay. There's a folding bed in there. And tomorrow morning – "

"No, I'll go right now. After all, everyone else seems to be leaving, don't they?"

"Yes, if they haven't already."

"So I think I'd better go as well. Thank you for letting me spend so many days with you. Really, I'm most grateful to you. There are many people who wouldn't have done it, you know. I'll remember it for a long time, a very long time."

He turned out to have a thick stick, which he must have cut in the forest the day before. His eyes met Maria Leonidovna's, and his look confused her.

"Wait a moment, I'll bring you something." She turned around and lightly stepped out.

"That's not necessary. I don't need anything," he shouted firmly. "Don't worry, please. Goodbye."

In the yard the men were tying something to the roof of the Kreins' car. She ran into the house, pulled fifty francs out of her purse, wrapped the remains of the roast beef and two rolls in a napkin, and went back to the one there now. He had left quietly, so that no one would notice, and very quickly. In the room it was as if he had never even stayed there; not a single object was out of place.

She looked around, as if he might still be standing somewhere in a corner. She walked out, went back in again, and then walked to the gate and opened it. Someone was walking alone down the lane – already quite a distance away. She watched him for a moment, and suddenly, for no reason, tears came to her eyes, and she couldn't see anything.

"He's leaving, he's leaving," she said very quietly but distinctly, the way people sometimes utter a meaningless word, and burst into tears. And without understanding what was wrong, or why she had suddenly been overcome by such weakness, she closed the gate gently and went into the house.

In the morning a life began that had nothing to do either with the departed guest or with Maria Leonidovna's secret thoughts. They loaded up the cars so that the spare tire bumped along behind them on the ground. They locked up the house and sat Kiryusha between his father and grandmother – that day he had exhibited the early signs of rebellion, and they were trying to conceal it. Edouard Zontag, in good form after a night's sleep, was worried that they hadn't taken enough gas. He took one more long look at the map before setting off. In the first car rode the Kreins and Maria Leonidovna. Manyura rattled on incessantly.

They drove through the deserted village slowly, with difficulty, the spare tire constantly bumping against the road. When they reached the forest, they started taking country lanes heading in the direction of Blois. They stopped by the chateau where Chabarov worked as a groundsman. The iron gates were wide open, and horses, still saddled, grazed on the English lawn between young cedars. A French squadron had been stationed there since the previous day. Soldiers were lying on the grass in front of the house, and on the ground floor a vast hall, with two rows of windows, and its candelabra, mirrors, and bronzes, could be glimpsed through the broken panes.

Chabarov came out wearing corduroy trousers and a matching jacket. The lower half of his face was covered with gray whiskers. Without even saying good-morning, he said that he couldn't leave, that he had to stay behind: the night before Daunou (who lived in a nearby hamlet) had been found dead. He had shot himself, and since there was no one left in the area to bury him, Chabarov had decided to bury the body in his garden.

"If these brave lads," he said gloomily, pointing to the soldiers, "stay until evening and I manage to dig a suitable hole, then they'll be my witnesses, and that's the best I can hope for. But if they set off before then I'll have to wait for the new authorities to get here. There's no civilian population left."

Everyone became very quiet as they said goodbye. Krein even got out of the car to embrace him. A minute later both cars drove off downhill, heavy with their loads, following each other closely.

That day, the sound of gunfire came from the other direction, from the northwest. In the sky, with a noise that had not been heard before, like a wail, swooped two German fighter planes.

First published in Russian: 1940
Translation by Marian Schwartz

NINA BERBEROVA

Неотвратимость музыки
Борис Слуцкий

Музыки бесполезные звуки,
лишние звуки,
неприменяемые тоны,
болью не вызванные стоны.

Не обоснована ведь ни бытом,
ни – даже страшно сказать – бытием
музыка!
Разве чем-то забытым,
чем-то, чего мы не сознаем.

Все-таки встаем и поем.
Все-таки идем и мурлычем.
Вилкой в розетку упрямо тычем,
чтоб разузнать о чем-то своем.

Inevitably, Music
Boris Slutsky

Music – what is it but useless sounds,
Superfluous sounds,
Tones with no aim to evoke them,
Moans with no pain to provoke them.

Not motivated by mere subsistence,
Nor (dare I say it?) defined by existence,
Music!
Memories lost in the distance,
Untouched by our conscious insistence.

Yet we sing and hum – the sound swells,
Try as we might, we can't block it.
We stubbornly poke the plug in the socket,
Trying to tease out some clue to ourselves.

First published in Russian: 1946
Translation by Lawrence Bogoslaw and Lydia Razran Stone

Pyotr Ilyich Tchaikovsky

Written in 1834 and published the next year in Gogol's collection of essays *Arabesques*, this brief statement compares and ranks the three titular arts. Curiously, Gogol pays little attention to verbal art, focusing instead on the transcendent qualities he sees in music.

Sculpture, Painting and Music
Nikolai Gogol

Let us praise the Creator of myriads for His kindness and mercy to mankind in sending us three wondrous sisters! They bring beauty and sweetness to our world. Without them the Earth would be a desert that tumbled along its way without song. Our desires are rendered more amicable and connected by their presence among us; let us raise the first goblet in honor of Sculpture! Sensuous and lovely, she was the first to visit the earth. A fleeting apparition, she is a vestige left behind of the people she contained within her, with all of its spirit and life. She is a visible phantom of that luminous Greek world that has receded from us into the profound depths of the ages and has already become shrouded in mist, and is accessible only to a poet's thoughts. This world is one entwined with grape clusters and olive vines, harmonious fantasies and luxurious paganism; a world that moves to a line of dancers whose Bacchic impulses are accompanied by the sound of tambourines; a world in which beauty has been suffused throughout: in the poor man's hovel, under a plane tree's branches, beneath marble columns, upon a plaza teeming with a lively, capricious people, in a relief that adorns a festival goblet and depicts an entire twisting chain of graceful mythology; where the goddess of beauty shyly emerges from the sea foam, where mermen speed by clapping their hands; and where Poseidon, silver and white, emerges from the depths of his splendid element; a world where all of religion is contained within beauty, human beauty, in a woman's deific beauty; this entire world has remained in her, in this tender Sculpture, and only she can so vividly express its luminous existence.

Pale and milky white, Sculpture exudes beauty, bliss, and, voluptuousness within its opaque marble. She has preserved a single idea, a single thought: beauty, the proud beauty of mankind. No matter how ardent its passions or how strong its impulses, in her the human figure is always marvelous, proud, and involuntarily assumes a pose both athletic and free. In her, everything merges into beauty and sensuality: the heart's suffering cry cannot be drawn out of the suffering figures; but rather, as it were, you enjoy their suffering. That is how much a sense of pliant and peaceful beauty subdues the strivings of the spirit within them. Sculpture has never expressed a mysterious feeling of infinite depth. She creates only quick movements: fierce anger, a sudden wail, horror, sudden fright, tears, pride and derision and, finally, beauty, submerged entirely within her. She transforms all the viewer's feelings into pure pleasure, a pleasure so peaceful it recreates the bliss and self-satisfaction of the pagan world. There are no secret, boundless feelings that bring endless dreams with them. In her you will not find an entire lifetime, filled with tempests and upheavals. She is splendidly fleeting, like a beauty who glances in the mirror, twinkles a smile at the sight of her reflection, and already dashing off, trailing a crowd of proud youths behind her. She is as enchanting as life, as the world, as the sensual beauty for which she forms an altar. Sculpture was born with the robustly formed pagan world. It expressed that world, and perished along with it. Vain was the desire to express the lofty phenomena of Christianity through Sculpture. She was as removed from it as the pagan faith itself. Never could elevated and expansive thoughts find rest upon on her voluptuous surface without being engulfed by her sensuality.

Not so her two sisters, Painting and Music, whom Christianity founded out of nothingness and transformed into something monumental. By that impulse they developed and expanded beyond the boundaries of the sensual world. I feel pity for my sculpture of cloud and marble! But shine still brighter, my goblet, in my humble cell, and long live Painting! Exalted and gorgeous, like autumn in its rich finery, flickering across the window sash, entwined with grapes, peaceful and vast like the universe, bright music for the eyes – you are splendid! Sculpture never dared express your heavenly revelations. It was never infused with those delicate, mystical characteristics that cause you to feel heaven filling your soul and sense the ineffable when you gaze upon them. Here, as though shrouded in mist, long galleries seem to present themselves, and you find yourself displayed, alive yet darkened from implacable time, inside antiquated gilded frames. Before you stands a speechless observer, arms crossed on his chest; his face displays not enjoyment, but a pleasure not of this world. You were not the achievement of a mere nation, but expressed all that is contained in the lofty and mystical Christian world. Look upon her, lost in thought, her splendid head resting upon her arm, her clear gaze so sustained and full of inspiration! She lengthens the moment, she expands life beyond the limits of the sensual, she purloins phenomena for which there are no words from the other world, a world without limits. Her inspired brush can depict everything imprecise that marble, hewn by a sculptor's mighty hammer, cannot. Painting, like Sculpture, also expresses passions everyone understands, yet sensuality does not predominate in them the same way; everything is suffused by the spiritual. Suffering is expressed more vividly, evokes compassion, and leads to sympathy rather than pleasure. Nor does Painting embrace mankind alone; for her limits are wider; she enfolds the entire world within herself; all the splendid phenomena that surround mankind are under her dominion; the entire secret harmony and the connection between man and nature reside within her alone. She unites the sensual and the spiritual.

But effervesce more vigorously, my third goblet! Sparkle more brightly and splash a sonorous foam upon its golden edges, for you sparkle in honor of music. She is more triumphant and impetuous than both of her sisters. She is made of impulse alone. At once she tears the ground from under a man's feet, deafening him with a roar of powerful sounds and immediately absorbing him into her world. She pounds his nerves like a keyboard, masterfully, through his entire essence and sets him aquiver. He is neither feeling pleasure nor suffering, but he himself is transformed into suffering. His soul is not beholding unfathomable phenomenon; his spirit is living them, living its own life, living its urges, living staggeringly and rebelliously. Unseen, like a siren, Music has suffused the whole world, flooded its banks, and breathes a thousand different forms. She is exhausting and rebellious, but all the more powerful and intense when streaming in a single harmonious movement beneath the endless, dark vaults of a cathedral where thousands of prostrate pilgrims have gathered, stripping bare their most intimate thoughts, circling in sorrow with them, and leaving behind a protracted silence and a lingering, fading sound that trembles far below its peaked tower.

How should one compare you, three splendid princesses of the world? Sensual and captivating, Sculpture produces pleasure, painting – quiet joy and dreaming, and music – passion and turbulence of the spirit. Gazing upon a marble work of Sculpture, the spirit is involuntarily enraptured; gazing upon a work of painting it assumes a meditative state; but in listening to music it becomes a painful wail, as if possessed by no desire but escape from the body. Music is ours! She belongs to the new world! She remained with us after sculpture, and painting, and architecture abandoned us. Never have we been so thirsty for impulses that move the spirit as in the present time, when a shower of petty whims and fancies, tales of which our nineteenth century is racking its brains over, is approaching and pressing upon us. Everything is conspiring against us; an entire tempting chain of sophisticated and luxurious inventions impels our feelings more and more toward silence and sleep. We thirst for salvation and escape from these terrible seducers, and throw ourselves into music. Please be our guardian angel and and savior! Do not leave us! Awaken our mercenary souls! Strike our slumbering feelings with even sharper sounds! Disturb, tear out, and chase away, even for an instant, that cold and horrid egoism that strives to possess our world. Under the powerful sweep of your bow let the thief's turbulent soul sense the pangs of conscience, even for the blink of an eye, let the speculator tear up his accounts, and shamelessness and impudence involuntarily squeeze out a tear in recognition of your talent. O, do not leave us, our Divinity! The great Creator of the world, in his vast wisdom, has vanquished us into a deepening silence: he bestowed the concept of architecture upon unevolved man. By force alone and without machines, he took over a hill of granite, piled it up into a sharp cliff toward the sky, and prostrated himself before its monstrous greatness. The Creator sent splendid Sculpture to the bright, ancient, sensual world, which introduced a pure and modest beauty, and the entire ancient world burned incense to beauty. The esthetic sense of beauty fused that world into a single harmony and restrained it from vulgar pleasures. It was to the centuries of disquiet and dark, where violence and falsehood often triumphed, where the demon of superstition and intolerance chased away everything brightly colored, that the Creator gave inspired Painting, which depicted unearthly phenomena and the heavenly pleasures enjoyed by charmers. But to our young and decaying age he sent down potent music in order to turn us sweepingly toward him. But if music were also to leave us, what then would become of our world?

First published in Russian: 1835
Translation by Deborah Hoffman

Аккорды
Константин Бальмонт

В красоте музыкальности,
Как в недвижной зеркальности,
Я нашёл очертания снов,
До меня не рассказанных,
Тосковавших и связанных,
Как растенья под глыбою льдов.

Я им дал наслаждение,
Красоту их рождения,
Я разрушил звенящие льды.
И, как гимны неслышные,
Дышат лотосы пышные
Над пространством зеркальной воды.

И в немой музыкальности,
В этой новой зеркальности,
Создаёт их живой хоровод
Новый мир, недосказанный,
Но с рассказанным связанный
В глубине отражающих вод.

Chords
Konstantin Balmont

Within music's perfection,
As in mirrored reflection,
I've discovered the outlines of dreams,
Before me unenvisioned,
Mired in longing, imprisoned,
Like lush lotus in ice covered streams.

They're reborn, liberated,
Full of beauty, elated.
I have shattered their ice chains – they're free.
So their green emanations,
Like mute hymns of salvation,
Waft above the clear surface to me.

Now mute music's perfection,
Living mirrored reflection,
Forms a chorus from which there will flow
A new world, still half mystery,
Yet arising from history
In the depths of the waters below.

First published in Russian: 1897
Translation by Lydia Razran Stone and Michael Ishenko

Mikhail Glinka while composing his opera, "Ruslan and Ludmila"
Ilya Repin (1887)

This selection is taken from *Russian Nights* (1844), a novel by Odoevsky that probes a great number of topics, genres, and philosophical questions. Odoevsky was a talented music critic in his own right and a huge proponent of the works of Mikhail Glinka.

The Sixth Night
Vladimir Odoyevsky

"Tell me," said Rostislav, as he came to Faust at the usual time of their discussions, "Why do you and all of us like to stay up late at night? Why is it that at night our concentration is more constant, thoughts are livelier, and our souls are more talkative?"

"It's easy to answer that question," said Vyacheslav. "General silence involuntarily disposes man to meditation."

ROSTISLAV: "General silence? Here? Where the real traffic in our city begins only by ten o'clock at night? And what sort of meditation is it? People simply congregate for some reason; that's why all gatherings, discussions, balls take place at night; it is as if man instinctively puts off his joining others till night. But why so?"

VICTOR: "It seems to me that that can be explained by a physiological phenomenon: it is well known that around midnight a sort of fever takes place in an organism – and in this state all nerves are excited, and what we take for liveliness of mind, talkativeness, is nothing but a result of our sickly state, a sort of delirium."

ROSTISLAV: "But you haven't answered my question: Why does this sickly state, as you say, make people congregate?"

FAUST: "If I were a scholar I would say to you, with Schelling, that from time immemorial night has been considered the oldest of beings and that it was not, for nothing that our ancestors, the Slavs, figured time by nights.[1] If I were a mystic I would explain this phenomenon to you quite simply. You see, night is the domain of a power hostile to man; people feel it, and in order to escape their enemy they unite, they look for support in one another: that's why people are more fearful at night; that's why ghost stories, stories about evil spirits, produce a stronger impression on them than in the daytime."

"And that's why people," added Vyacheslav laughing, "try very hard to kill the hostile power by playing cards; and Carsel's lamp chases away goblins."

"You won't stop mystics with this mockery," said Faust. "They will reply to you that the hostile power has two profound and clever ideas: the first – it tries to convince man with all its might that it does not exist, and therefore it suggests to him every possible means of forgetting it; and the second – to equalize people as much as possible, to unite them so that not one head, not one heart should stand out; cards are one of the means the hostile power employs to achieve this double purpose. First, while playing cards one can't think of anything else but cards, and second, all are made equal during a card game: both the superior and his subordinate, handsome and ugly-looking man, a scholar and an ignoramus, a genius and a cipher, an intelligent man and a fool; there is no distinction between them: the worst fool can win from the greatest philosopher on earth, and a minor employee from a great nobleman. Imagine to yourself the delight of some cipher when he can win from Newton, or say to Leibnitz: 'But, sir, you don't know how to play; you, Mr. Leibnitz, don't know how to hold cards!' That's Jacobinism at its height. Meanwhile, the hostile power profits also from the fact that during a card game, under the cover of an innocent entertainment, almost all vices of man are encouraged secretly: envy, anger,

VLADIMIR ODOYEVSKY

....

1. See Schelling's small yet amazing work in its depth and scholarship, *Uber die Gottheiten von Samothrace* (Stuttgart, 1815), p. 12. [Author's note]

self-interest, vengeance, cunning, deceit – everything on a small scale; nevertheless, one's soul gets to know them, and that is of great advantage to the hostile power."

"Well, can't we do without mysticism?" Vyacheslav finally interjected, losing his patience.

"I'll spare you gladly," answered Faust.

"And yet my question has remained unanswered," Rostislav noted.

FAUST: "You know my unalterable conviction that man, even if he can answer some question, can never translate it correctly into ordinary language. In cases like that I always look for some object in external nature which, by analogy, could serve at least as an approximate expression of the thought. Have you ever noticed that long before sunset, especially in our northern skies, down at the horizon, behind distant clouds, a crimson strip unlike an evening glow appears, while the sun is still shining in all its brightness? That is part of dawn to people in the other hemisphere. Consequently, each minute there is dawn upon the earth and each minute a part of its inhabitants, like an ordinary sentry, rises to its post. Providence arranged it so purposely: perhaps this phenomenon tells us clearly that nature may not take advantage of man's sleep for a moment, since all nature's harmful influence upon man's organism really increases at night: plants do not purify the air but spoil it; dew assumes harmful properties; an experienced doctor watches over his patient predominantly at night, when any disease becomes worse. Maybe we should follow the doctor's example and observe our diseased soul, as he observes a diseased body, just at the moment when the organism undergoes harmful influences most of all. The sun is more favorable to man: it is the symbol of some sort of preference shown to him; it disperses harmful mists; it makes coarse plants process the living part of the air for man.[2] He invigorates man's heart, and perhaps that is why his sleep is so sweet at sunrise: he feels the symbol of his ally and peacefully falls asleep under his warm and light cover."

....

2. It is known that the green parts of plants exhale oxygen, but only under the light of the sun. [Author's note]

VICTOR: "Oh, you dreamer! Facts are nothing to you. Doesn't man suffer from the sun's heat, like all plants?"

FAUST: "I assure you that my facts are more reliable than yours, perhaps because they are less tangible. Yes, the sun's heat is unbearable for man! But this fact contains another, namely, that the sun does not affect us directly but through the coarse atmosphere of the earth. Aeronauts did not feel the heat when they rose into the upper layers of the air. To me this is an important proof: the higher we are from the earth, the less we are affected by its nature."

VICTOR: "That's completely true, and here is another proof: beyond a certain limit of the atmosphere, blood came out of the aeronauts' ears; it became difficult for them to breathe; and they shivered from cold."

ROSTISLAV: "This fact, it seems to me, expresses the real and difficult problem of man: to rise from the earth, without leaving it."

VYACHESLAV: "That is, in other words, one must seek for the possible – and not chase in vain after the impossible."

Faust answered nothing but changed the subject.

"We won't be able to outargue one another till dawn," he said, "but, although you are my friends, I will not let you deprive me of my sweet morning sleep for anything. Should we proceed with the manuscript? After all, we must finish it."

Faust began: "In the numbered order *The Economist* is followed by *Beethoven's Last Quartet:*

I was convinced that Krespel had become insane. The professor maintained the contrary. "Nature and special circumstances," he said, "have removed from some people the mask behind which we indulge in all kinds of absurdities. They are like insects whose tissue an anatomist removes, thereby revealing the movement of their muscles." Krespel puts into action what we merely think.

Hoffmann

In the spring of 1827, in one of the houses on the outskirts of Vienna, a few music lovers were practicing Beethoven's new quartet that had just been published. With amazement and annoyance they followed the formless outbursts of the enfeebled genius: his idiom had changed so much! Gone was the charm of an original melody, full of poetic concepts; the artistic touch had been replaced by the painstaking pedantry of an inept counterpointist; the fire that formerly blazed up in his fast allegros and, gradually growing, poured out like burning lava in full, great harmonies had died down amidst incomprehensible dissonances; the original, humorous themes of the gay minuet had changed into leaps and trills impossible on any instrument. Everywhere there were immature, vain attempts to create effects that do not exist in music. Yet that was the same Beethoven, the one whose name, along with the names of Haydn and Mozart, the Teuton utters full of rapture and pride! Often led to despair by the absurdity of the piece, the musicians would throw down their bows and were on the point of asking if this was not a mockery of the creations of the immortal one? Some ascribed the decline to his loss of hearing, which had afflicted him in the last years of his life; others, to his insanity, which sometimes overshadowed his creative talent; some expressed false regrets, and a scoffer remembered an incident during the concert when Beethoven's last symphony was performed, when he waved his hands completely off beat, as if he were conducting the orchestra, without even noticing that the real conductor was standing behind him. But soon they would pick up their bows again, and out of respect for the former glory of the famous creator of symphonies, and as if against their own will, they continued playing his incomprehensible work.

Suddenly the door opened and in came a man in a black suit, without a tie, his hair tousled; his eyes were aflame – but this was not the flame of a genius; only the low-hanging, sharply cut extremities of his forehead showed an unusual development of the musical organ, which once so delighted Hall, when he examined Mozart's head.

"Pardon me, gentlemen," said the unexpected guest, "allow me to have a look at your apartment… it is for rent…"

Then, with his hands folded behind his back, he approached the musicians. He was offered a seat respectfully; he sat there, inclining his head now to one side, now to the other, trying to hear the music, but in vain, and tears came streaming from his eyes. Quietly he left the performers and took a seat in a remote corner of the room, covering his face with his hands. But no sooner had the bow of the first violinist sounded upon touching the string near the bridge while playing an incidental note added to the seventh, and a wild harmony resounded in the doubled notes of the other instruments, than the poor man started and shouted: "I can hear! I can hear!" – and wild with joy he began clapping his hands and stamping his feet.

"Ludwig!" said the young girl, who had followed him into the room. "Ludwig! It's time to go home. We are in the way here!"

He glanced at the girl, understood her, and followed her without a word, like a child.

On the outskirts of the city, on the fourth floor of an old house, there is a little stuffy room, divided by a partition. Its only adornments are a bed covered by a torn blanket, several rolls of music paper, and the remnants of a piano. This was the abode, this was the world, of the immortal Beetho-

VLADIMIR ODOYEVSKY

ven. He did not utter a word all the way. But when they reached the room, Ludwig sat down on his bed, took the girl's hand into his, and said:

"My kind Louise! Only you understand me; only you are not afraid of me; you are the only one I don't disturb... Do you think that all these gentlemen who play my music understand me? Nothing of the sort! Not one of the local conductors even knows how to conduct it; all they care for is that the orchestra plays in time; music doesn't concern them! They think I'm growing weak. I even noticed that some of them seemed to smile while playing my quartet; that's a true sign that they never understood me. On the contrary, I have only now become a true and great musician. On the way home, I conceived a symphony that will immortalize my name; I'll write it and burn all the former ones. In it I'll change all the laws of harmony; I'll find effects no one has suspected until now. I'll build it on a chromatic melody and use twenty kettledrums; into it I'll introduce hundreds of chimes tuned to various pitches, because," he added in a whisper, "I'll tell you a secret: when you took me to the belfry, I discovered that chimes are the most harmonious instrument, and can be used successfully in a quiet *adagio*. Into the finale I'll introduce drumbeats and gunshots – and I will hear this symphony, Louise!" he shouted, beside himself with rapture. "I hope I'll hear it," he added, smiling after a moment's reflection. "Do you remember, in Vienna, in the presence of all the crowned heads of the world, I conducted, the orchestra in my "Battle of Waterloo"? Thousands of musicians, obeying the wave of my hand, twelve conductors, and all around, the gunfire and cannon shots... Oh! that's my best work to date, despite that pedant Weber.[3] But what I am going to create now will overshadow even that work. I cannot refrain from giving you an idea of it."

With these words Beethoven went up to the piano, which did not have a single string intact, and with an air of dignity began playing on the dead keys. They hit the dry wood of the broken instrument monotonously, while

---

3. Gottfried Weber, the well-known contrapuntist of our time, who should not be mistaken for the composer of *Freischütz*, quite strongly and justly criticized *Wellington's Victory,* the weakest of Beethoven's compositions, in his interesting and scholarly journal *Cecilia*. [Author's note]

the most elaborate fugues in five and six voices passed through all the mysteries of counterpoint, obediently, and as if on their own, taking shape under the fingers of the creator of the music to *Egmont,* and he himself tried to give his music as much expression as he could... Suddenly, powerfully, he struck the keys with his whole hand, and stopped.

"Do you hear?" he asked Louise. "Here is a chord no one has dared to use until now. That's it! I shall combine all the tones of the chromatic scale in one chord and I shall prove to the pedants that this chord is correct. But I don't hear it, Louise; I don't hear it! Do you understand what it means not to hear one's own music? And yet, when I gather all the wild sounds into one chord, it seems to me as if they do resound in my ear. And the more depressed I feel, Louise, the more notes I want to add to a seventh, the true essence of which no one has perceived before me... But enough of that! Maybe I have bored you as I have bored everybody else? Now, do you know what? For such a wonderful invention I should reward myself today with a glass of wine. How do you like the idea, Louise?"

Tears came to the eyes of the poor girl, who alone of all Beethoven's pupils did not leave him and who provided for his livelihood by the work of her hands, under the pretext of taking lessons with him. She added to the scanty income Beethoven received for his works, most of which had been spent senselessly, moving from one apartment to another, and giving money away to anyone who cared to ask for it. There was no wine! There were barely a few pennies left for bread... But, turning her head away from Ludwig, so as to hide her confusion, she poured a glass of water and gave it to Beethoven.

"What an excellent Rhine wine!" he said, sipping from the glass with the air of a connoisseur, "A regal Rhine wine! Just like the one from the wine cellar of my late father Frederick, God bless his soul. I remember this wine very well. It improves from day to day, as a good wine should!" And with these words, in a hoarse but firm voice, he began to sing his music to the famous song of Goethe's Mephistopheles:

"Es war einmal ein Konig
Der hatt eine grosse Floh,"

but involuntarily he kept changing it to the mysterious melody by which Beethoven explained Mignon.[4]

"Listen, Louise," he said finally, returning the glass to her, "the wine has given me strength now, and I intend to tell you something which, for a very long time, I've been of two minds about telling you. You know, it seems to me that I won't live long now – and what kind of life do I lead? It is a chain of infinite torments. In the earliest days of my youth, I became aware of the abyss that separated thought from expression. Alas, I was never able to express my soul; I was never able to put on paper what my imagination told me. I wrote, people played it – it was never the same!… It was not only not what I had been feeling; it was not even what I had written. Here, a melody was lost because it had not occurred to a lowly craftsman to put in an extra valve; there, an intolerable bassoonist made me rewrite a whole symphony because his bassoon couldn't play a couple of bass notes; there, the violinist did away with a necessary sound in the chord because it was difficult for him to take double stops. And the voices, the singing, the rehearsals-of oratorios, of operas?… Oh, that inferno! It still sounds in my ears! But I was still happy then. Sometimes I would see the insensible musicians become inspired; I would hear in their sounds something like a dark thought that had sunk in my imagination: then I would be beside myself, dissolved in the harmony I myself had created. But the time came when my sensitive ear gradually became coarse: it was still sensitive enough to hear the mistakes musicians made, but it was closed to beauty, a dark cloud enveloped it – and now I can't hear my works anymore, I can't hear them, Louise!… Whole series of harmonic chords float in my imagination; original melodies cross each other, fusing in a mysterious unity; I want to express it,

4. Kennst du das Land... etc. (Knowest thou the land, etc.)

but everything disappears: stubborn reality won't emit a single sound for me – coarse feelings destroy all my soul's activity. Oh, what can be more horrible than this strife between the soul and feelings, between soul and soul? To engender an artistic creation in your mind and to die hourly in the torments of giving birth!... This is the death of a soul! How terrible, how full of life is this death!

"And what's more, this insensate Gottfried involves me in these sense-less musical arguments, compels me to explain why I used such and such a combination of melodies, or such and such a combination of instruments in one place or another, when I cannot explain it even to myself! As if these people knew what the soul of a musician is, what the soul of a man is! They think one can pattern it as a craftsman patterns his instruments, all according to the rules invented at his leisure by the dried-out brain of a theoretician...No, when the moment of rapture overcomes me, I become convinced that art can no longer remain in such a false state; that new, fresh forms will take the place of decayed ones; that all the present instruments will be abandoned and will be replaced by others which will perform the works of talented men perfectly; that the absurd disparity between written music and the music heard will finally disappear.

"I spoke to our gentlemen the professors about it, but they did not understand me, as they did not understand the power of rapture given to the artist, as they did not understand that I am forestalling time and acting in accordance with laws of nature as yet unnoticed by ordinary men and at times incomprehensible even to myself... Fools! In their cold rapture, in their moments of leisure, they choose a theme; they develop and expand it and do not even fail to repeat it in another key; or in someplace they indicate wind instruments, or some strange chord over which they ponder again and again, and they polish and refine it all so sensibly. What do they want? I can't work that way... They compare me to Michelangelo – but how did the creator of 'Moses' work? In anger, in rage, with powerful strokes of his hammer he hit the motionless marble and made it impart a living idea, hidden beneath the stone. This is how I work too! I do not understand cold rapture! I understand only the kind of rapture when the whole world turns into harmony for me, when every feeling, every thought sounds within me; when all the forces of nature become my instruments; when blood boils in my veins, my body shivers, and my hair stands on end… And all is in vain! And what is the sense of it all? What is the purpose? You live, you suffer, you think; you write it down and that's the end of it: the sweet agonies of creation are chained to the sheet of paper – you can't make them come back! The thoughts of a proud creative spirit are humiliated and imprisoned, the lofty effort of the earthly creator, challenging the force of nature, becomes the work of human hands! And people! They come, they listen – as if they were judges, as if you had been creating for them! What do they care that a thought which has assumed an image understandable to them is only a link in the infinite chain of thoughts and sufferings, that the moment when the artist descends to the level of man is only a fragment of the long and painful life of immeasurable feeling; that each of his expressions, each line was born out of the bitter tears of a Seraph who is imprisoned in human flesh and who would give half of his life for a moment of the fresh air of inspiration? And then the time comes, as it did just now, when you feel that your soul has burnt out, your forces have weakened, your head is in pain; your thoughts become confused and everything is covered with a veil… Oh, Louise, I wish I could reveal to you my last thoughts and feelings, which I keep and guard in the treasury of my soul… But, what do I hear?"

With these words Beethoven jumped up and with a powerful blow of his hand opened the window, through which harmonious sounds were floating in from the neighboring house…

"I hear!" shouted Beethoven, throwing himself on his knees, full of tender emotion, stretching his hands toward the open window. "This is Egmont's symphony – yes, I recognize it: here are the wild battle cries, here the storm of passions; they flare up, they seethe; here they are at their fullest – and everything is quiet again; only the vigil light is left gleaming, but it is dimming, dying, but not forever… Trumpets sound again: they fill the entire world, and no one can silence them…

Crowds of people were coming and going at a splendid ball given by one of the ministers in Vienna.

"What a pity!" someone said. "The theater conductor Beethoven has died, and they say that there is no money for his burial."

But the voice was lost in the crowd: everyone was listening attentively to the words of two diplomats discussing an argument that had taken place between some people at the court of a German prince.

"I should like to know," said Victor, "to what extent this anecdote is true."

"I cannot give you a satisfactory answer to that," said Faust, "and the owners of the manuscript would hardly have been able to answer your question because, it seems to me, they weren't acquainted with the methods of those historians who read only what is written in a biography and refuse to read what is not written in it. Apparently they reasoned thus: If this anecdote was really true, all the better; if it was invented by someone, it means that it happened in the heart of the writer; consequently, this event *was,* although it didn't *happen.* Such a view may seem strange, but in this case my friends seem to have followed the example of mathematicians, who in higher calculations do not worry whether 2 and 3 or 4 and 10 were ever united in nature, but daringly conceive the equation a + b as all possible combinations of numbers. However, constant moving from place to place, deafness, a kind of madness, constant dissatisfaction – all these belonged to the so-called historical facts of Beethoven's life; except that honest writers of biographical articles, for lack of documents, didn't undertake to explain the connection between his deafness and madness, between his madness and dissatisfaction, between his dissatisfaction and his music."

VYACHESLAV: "What need had they! Whether a fact is true or false, for me it expresses, as Rostislav said, my constant conviction, which I mentioned

VLADIMIR ODOYEVSKY

at the beginning of the evening, namely: man should limit himself to the possible, or, as Voltaire said in his answer to a moral axiom: *Cela est bien dit; mais il faut cultiver notre jardin.*[5]

FAUST: "That means that Voltaire didn't even believe what he wanted to believe."

ROSTISLAV: "One thing struck me in this anecdote – the inexpressibility of our sufferings. Indeed, the most cruel, the clearest torments for us are those we cannot communicate. Whoever is capable of communicating his sufferings has already halfway rid himself of them."

VICTOR: "You, my dreamer friends, have thought of a nice trick: in order to get rid of positive questions you tried to convince us that human language is inadequate to express our thoughts and feelings. It seems to me that it is rather our knowledge that is inadequate. If man were to devote himself to pure, simple observation of coarse nature, which you try to keep in the background – but, please note, to *pure* observation, eliminating all his own thoughts and feelings, every internal operation – then he would be able to understand both himself and nature much more clearly and he would find enough expressions for himself even in an ordinary language."

FAUST: "I don't know if this so-called pure observation doesn't contain an optical illusion; I don't know if man can completely separate from himself all *his own* thoughts and feelings, all his own *recollections,* so that nothing of his *I* would enter his observations; the very thought of observing without thinking is in itself a theory *a priori*… But we have strayed from Beethoven. No one's music impresses me so much as Beethoven's. It seems to touch every string of the heart; it raises in it all the forgotten, most secret sufferings and gives them shape; Beethoven's joyful themes are even more horrible; in them someone seems to laugh – out of despair. It is a strange thing: any other music, particularly that of Haydn, creates a pleasant, soothing impression in me. The effect Beethoven's music has is much stronger, but it disturbs you: through its wonderful harmony you hear some inhar-

---

5. *Candide.*

monious cry. You listen to a symphony of his, and you are enraptured – yet your soul languishes. I'm sure that Beethoven's music must have been a torment to himself.

"Once, at a time when I did not yet have any idea of the composer's life, I told a passionate admirer of Haydn about this strange effect Beethoven's music had upon me. 'I understand you,' replied the Haydnist. 'The reason for this effect is the reason why Beethoven, despite his musical genius (perhaps a higher genius than Haydn's), was never able to write spiritual music that would come close to the oratorios of the latter.' 'Why so?' I asked. 'Because,' answered the Haydnist, 'Beethoven did not believe in what Haydn believed.'"

VICTOR: "So! I expected that! Yes, tell me, gentlemen, what pleasure do you find in mixing things that have nothing in common? How can man's convictions influence music, poetry, science? It is difficult to speak about such subjects, but it seems obvious to me that if something extraneous can affect aesthetic works, then it is perhaps only the degree of knowledge. Knowledge, obviously, may extend the circle of the artist's vision; he must feel roomier within it. But how he came to this knowledge, in what way, dark or light, doesn't concern poetry. Recently someone had the happy idea of making up a new science – physical philosophy or philosophical physics – the purpose of which would be *to affect morality by means of knowledge*[6] – this, in my opinion, is one of the most useful undertakings of our time."

FAUST: "I know that this opinion is now triumphing. But, tell me, why wouldn't anyone ask a doctor who is known to be an inveterate atheist to the bedside of a sick man? What does there seem to be in common between a medical formula and a man's convictions? I agree with you in one thing: in the necessity of knowledge. Thus, for example, contrary to general opinion, I am convinced that a poet needs physical sciences; it is useful for him to descend sometimes to external nature, if only to convince him-

VLADIMIR ODOYEVSKY

---

6. In this spirit the journal *l'Educateur* by Mr. Rocour was published. [Author's note]

self of the superiority of his inner nature, and also to see that, to man's shame, letters in the book of nature are not as changeable and vague as in a human language. Letters there are constant, *stereotyped*. A poet can read in them much of what is important, but to do this he has to make sure he has good *glasses*... However, my friends, sunrise is near. 'It's time for us to calm down, dear Eunom,' as Paracelsus says in one of his forgotten folios."

First published in Russian: 1831
Translation by Olga Koshansky-Oleinikov and Ralph Matlaw

THE SIXTH NIGHT

Бетховен
Николай Заболоцкий

В тот самый день, когда твои созвучья
Преодолели сложный мир труда,
Свет пересилил свет, прошла сквозь тучу туча,
Гром двинулся на гром, в звезду вошла звезда.

И яростным охвачен вдохновеньем,
В оркестрах гроз и трепете громов,
Поднялся ты по облачным ступеням
И прикоснулся к музыке миров.

Дубравой труб и озером мелодий
Ты превозмог нестройный ураган,
И крикнул ты в лицо самой природе,
Свой львиный лик просунув сквозь орган.

И пред лицом пространства мирового
Такую мысль вложил ты в этот крик,
Что слово с воплем вырвалось из слова
И стало музыкой, венчая львиный лик.

В рогах быка опять запела лира,
Пастушьей флейтой стала кость орла,
И понял ты живую прелесть мира
И отделил добро его от зла.

И сквозь покой пространства мирового
До самых звезд прошел девятый вал...
Откройся, мысль! Стань музыкою, слово,
Ударь в сердца, чтоб мир торжествовал!

Beethoven
Nikolai Zabolotsky

That very day, when your concordant sounds
at last surmounted work's elaborate world,
light overpowered light, cloud passed through cloud,
storm stormed on storm, star penetrated star.

And in the grip of violent inspiration,
in orchestras of thunder loud and fierce,
you climbed the sky, station by cloudy station,
and laid your hands upon the music of the spheres.

With lakes of melody and with an organ's orchard,
you tamed the hurricane of dissonance,
daring to shout into the face of nature,
thrusting your lion's mien through organ-pipes.

Before the face of all the earthly world,
you put such thought into that shout of yours,
that, with a cry, word tore itself from word
and, turned to music, crowned your lion's face.

A lyre sang again between a bull's long horns,
the eagle's bone became a shepherd's flute,
you understood the living beauty of existence,
distinguishing its evil from its good.

And, through the calmness of the earthly world,
the ninth wave reached the very stars themselves…
Thought, bare yourself! Turn into music, word –
beat in our hearts, and give us reason to rejoice!

First published in Russian: 1946
Translation by Boris Dralyuk

Sergei Rachmaninov

In this short story, Nabokov's protagonist, Victor, encounters his ex-wife at a concert. Despite his proclamation that he has "no ear for music," the experience awakens profound memories and feelings in him, as the music acts a shield from the chaos of the everyday world.

Music

Vladimir Nabokov

The entrance hall overflowed with coats of both sexes; from the drawing room came a rapid succession of piano notes. Victor's reflection in the hall mirror straightened the knot of a reflected tie. Straining to reach up, the maid hung his overcoat, but it broke loose, taking down two others with it, and she had to begin all over again.

Already walking on tiptoe, Victor reached the drawing room, whereupon the music at once became louder and manlier. At the piano sat Wolf, a rare guest in that house. The rest – some thirty people in all – were listening in a variety of attitudes, some with chin propped on fist, others sending cigarette smoke up toward the ceiling, and the uncertain lighting lent a vaguely picturesque quality to their immobility: From afar, the lady of the house, with an eloquent smile, indicated to Victor an unoccupied seat, a pretzel-backed little armchair almost in the shadow of the grand piano. He responded with self-effacing gestures – it's all right, it's all right, I can stand; presently, however, he began moving in the suggested direction, cautiously sat down, and cautiously folded his arms. The performer's wife, her mouth half-open, her eyes blinking fast, was about to turn the page; now she has turned it. A black forest of ascending notes, a slope, a gap, then a separate group of little trapezists in flight. Wolf had long, fair eyelashes; his translucent ears were of a delicate crimson hue; he struck the keys with extraordinary velocity and vigor and, in the lacquered depths of the open keyboard lid, the doubles of his hands were engaged in a ghostly, intricate, even somewhat clownish mimicry.

To Victor any music he did not know – and all he knew was a dozen conventional tunes – could be likened to the patter of a conversation in a strange tongue: in vain you strive to define at least the limits of the words, but everything slips and merges, so that the laggard ear begins to feel boredom. Victor tried to concentrate on listening, but soon caught himself watching Wolf's hands and their spectral reflections. When the sounds grew into insistent thunder, the performer's neck would swell, his widespread fingers tensed, and he emitted a faint grunt. At one point his wife got ahead of him; he arrested the page with an instant slap of his open left palm, then with incredible speed himself flipped it over, and already both hands were fiercely kneading the compliant keyboard again. Victor made a detailed study of the man: sharp-tipped nose, jutting eyelids, scar left by a boil on his neck, hair resembling blond fluff, broad-shouldered cut of black jacket. For a moment Victor tried to attend to the music again, but scarcely had he focused on it when his attention dissolved. He slowly turned away, fishing out his cigarette case, and began to examine the other guests. Among the strange faces he discovered some familiar ones – nice, chubby Kocharovsky over there – should I nod to him? He did, but overshot his mark: it was another acquaintance, Shmakov, who acknowledged the nod: I heard he was leaving Berlin for Paris – must ask him about it. On a divan, flanked by two elderly ladies, corpulent, red-haired Anna Samoylovna, half-reclined with closed eyes, while her husband, a throat specialist, sat with his elbow propped on the arm of his chair. What is that glittering object he twirls in the fingers of his free hand? Ah yes, a pince-nez on a Chekhovian ribbon. Further, one shoulder in shadow, a hunchbacked, bearded man known to be a lover of music listened intently, an index finger stretched up against his temple. Victor could never remember his name and patronymic. Boris?

No, that wasn't it. Borisovich? Not that either. More faces. Wonder if the
Haruzins are here. Yes, there they are. Not looking my way. And in the next
instant, immediately behind them, Victor saw his former wife.

At once he lowered his gaze, automatically tapping his cigarette to dis-
lodge the ash that had not yet had time to form. From somewhere low
down his heart rose like a fist to deliver an uppercut, drew back, struck
again, then went into a fast, disorderly throb, contradicting the music and
drowning it. Not knowing which way to look, he glanced askance at the
pianist, but did not hear a sound: Wolf seemed to be pounding a silent
keyboard. Victor's chest got so constricted that he had to straighten up and
draw a deep breath; then, hastening back from a great distance, gasping for
air, the music returned to life, and his heart resumed beating with a more
regular rhythm.

They had separated two years before, in another town, where the sea
boomed at night, and where they had lived since their marriage. With his
eyes still cast down, he tried to ward off the thunder and rush of the past
with trivial thoughts: for instance, that she must have observed him a few
moments ago as, with long, noiseless, bobbing strides, he had tiptoed
the whole length of the room to reach this chair. It was as if someone
had caught him undressed or engaged in some idiotic occupation; and,
while recalling how in his innocence he had glided and plunged under
her gaze (hostile? derisive? curious?), he interrupted himself to consider
if his hostess or anyone else in the room might be aware of the situation,
and how had she got here, and whether she had come alone or with her
new husband, and what he, Victor, ought to do: stay as he was or look
her way? No, looking was still impossible; first he had to get used to her
presence in this large but confining room – for the music had fenced
them in and had become for them a kind of prison, where they were both
fated to remain captive until the pianist ceased constructing and keeping
up his vaults of sound.

What had he had time to observe in that brief glance of recognition a
moment ago? So little: her averted eyes, her pale cheek, a lock of black hair,

and, as a vague secondary character, beads or something around her neck. So little! Yet that careless sketch, that half-finished image already *was* his wife, and its momentary blend of gleam and shade already formed the unique entity which bore her name.

How long ago it all seemed! He had fallen madly in love with her one sultry evening, under a swooning sky, on the terrace of the tennis-club pavilion, and, a month later, on their wedding night, it rained so hard you could not hear the sea. What bliss it had been. Bliss – what a moist, lapping, and plashing word, so alive, so tame, smiling and crying all by itself. And the morning after: those glistening leaves in the garden, that almost noiseless sea, that languid, milky, silvery sea.

Something had to be done about his cigarette butt. He turned his head, and again his heart missed a beat. Someone had stirred, blocking his view of her almost totally, and was taking out a handkerchief as white as death; but presently the stranger's elbow would go and she would reappear, yes, in a moment she would reappear. No, I can't bear to look. There's an ashtray on the piano.

The barrier of sounds remained just as high and impenetrable. The spectral hands in their lacquered depths continued to go through the same contortions. "We'll be happy forever" – what melody in that phrase, what shimmer! She was velvet-soft all over, one longed to gather her up the way one could gather up a foal and its folded legs. Embrace her and fold her. And then what? What could one do to possess her completely? I love your liver, your kidneys, your blood cells. To this she would reply, "Don't be disgusting." They lived neither in luxury nor in poverty, and went swimming in the sea almost all year round. The jellyfish, washed up onto the shingly beach, trembled in the wind. The Crimean cliffs glistened in the spray. Once they saw fishermen carrying away the body of a drowned man; his bare feet, protruding from under the blanket, looked surprised. In the evenings she used to make cocoa.

He looked again. She was now sitting with downcast eyes, legs crossed, chin propped upon knuckles: she was very musical, Wolf must be playing some famous, beautiful piece. I won't be able to sleep for several nights, thought Victor as he contemplated her white neck and the soft angle of her knee. She wore a flimsy black dress, unfamiliar to him, and her necklace kept catching the light. No, I won't be able to sleep, and I shall have to stop coming here. It has all been in vain: two years of straining and struggling, my peace of mind almost regained – now I must start all over again, trying to forget everything, everything that had already been almost forgotten, plus this evening on top of it. It suddenly seemed to him that she was looking at him furtively and he turned away.

The music must be drawing to a close. When they come, those stormy, gasping chords, it usually signifies that the end is near. Another intriguing word, *end*... Rend, impend... Thunder rending the sky, dust clouds of impending doom. With the coming of spring she became strangely unresponsive. She spoke almost without moving her lips. He would ask, "What is the matter with you?" "Nothing. Nothing in particular." Sometimes she would stare at him out of narrowed eyes, with an enigmatic expression. "What *is* the matter?" "Nothing." By nightfall she would be as good as dead. You could not do anything with her, for, despite her being a small, slender woman, she would grow heavy and unwieldy, and as if made of stone. "Won't you finally tell me what is the matter with you?" So it went for almost a month. Then, one morning – yes, it was the morning of her birthday – she said quite simply, as if she were talking about some trifle, "Let's separate for a while. We can't go on like this." The neighbors' little daughter burst into the room to show her kitten (the sole survivor of a litter that had been drowned). "Go away, go away, later." The little girl left. There was a long silence. After a while, slowly, silently, he began twisting her wrists – he longed to break all of her, to dislocate all her joints with loud cracks. She started to cry. Then he sat down at the table and pretended to read the newspaper. She went out into the garden, but soon returned. "I can't keep it back any longer. I have to tell you everything." And with an odd astonishment, as if discussing another woman, and being astonished at her, and inviting him to share her astonishment, she told it, told it all. The man in question was a burly, modest, and reserved fellow; he used to come for a game of whist, and liked to talk about artesian wells. The first time had been in the park, then at his place.

The rest is all very vague. I paced the beach till nightfall. Yes, the music does seem to be ending. When I slapped his face on the quay, he said, "You'll pay dearly for this," picked up his cap from the ground, and walked away. I did not say good-bye to her. How silly it would have been to think of killing her. Live on, live. Live as you are living now; as you are sitting now, sit like that forever. Come, look at me, I implore you, please, please look. I'll forgive you everything, because someday we must all die, and then we shall know everything, and everything will be forgiven – so why put it off? Look at me, look at me, turn your eyes, *my* eyes, my darling eyes. No. Finished.

The last many-clawed, ponderous chords – another, and just enough breath left for one more, and, after this concluding chord, with which the music seemed to have surrendered its soul entirely, the performer took aim and, with feline precision, struck one simple, quite separate little golden note. The musical barrier dissolved. Applause. Wolf said, "It's been a very long time since I last played this." Wolf's wife said, "It's been a long time, you know, since my husband last played this piece." Advancing upon him, crowding him, nudging him with his paunch, the throat specialist said to Wolf: "Marvelous! I have always maintained that's the best thing he ever wrote. I think that toward the end you modernize the color of sound just a bit too much. I don't know if I make myself clear, but, you see – "

Victor was looking in the direction of the door. There, a slightly built, black-haired lady with a helpless smile was taking leave of the hostess, who kept exclaiming in surprise, "I won't hear of it, we're all going to have tea now, and then we're going to hear a singer." But she kept on smiling help-lessly and made her way to the door, and Victor realized that the music, which before had seemed a narrow dungeon where, shackled together by the resonant sounds, they had been compelled to sit face-to-face some twenty feet apart, had actually been incredible bliss, a magic glass dome that had embraced and imprisoned him and her, had made it possible for him to breathe the same air as she; and now everything had been broken and scattered, she was disappearing through the door, Wolf had shut the piano, and the enchanting captivity could not be restored.

She left. Nobody seemed to have noticed anything. He was greeted by a man named Boke who said in a gentle voice, "I kept watching you. What a reaction to music! You know, you looked so bored I felt sorry for you. Is it possible that you are so completely indifferent to it?"

"Why, no. I wasn't bored," Victor answered awkwardly. "It's just that I have no ear for music, and that makes me a poor judge. By the way, what was it he played?"

"What you will," said Boke in the apprehensive whisper of a rank outsider. " 'A Maiden's Prayer,' or the 'Kreutzer Sonata.' Whatever you will."

First published: 1932

The Green Violinist
Marc Chagall (1924)

Rothschild's Fiddle
Anton Chekhov

It was a tiny town, worse than a village, inhabited chiefly by old people who so seldom died that it was really vexatious. Very few coffins were
needed for the hospital and the jail; in a word, business was bad. If Yakov
Ivanov had been a maker of coffins in the county town, he would probably have owned a house of his own by now, and would have been called
Mr. Ivanov, but here in this little place he was simply called Yakov, and
for some reason his nickname was Bronze. He lived as poorly as any
common peasant in a little old hut of one room, in which he and Martha,
and the stove, and a double bed, and the coffins, and his joiner's bench,
and all the necessities of housekeeping were stowed away.

The coffins made by Yakov were serviceable and strong. For the peasants and townsfolk he made them to fit himself and never went wrong,
for, although he was seventy years old, there was no man, not even in the
prison, any taller or stouter than he was. For the gentry and for women
he made them to measure, using an iron yardstick for the purpose. He
was always very reluctant to take orders for children's coffins, and made
them contemptuously without taking any measurements at all, always
saying when he was paid for them:

"The fact is, I don't like to be bothered with trifles."

Beside what he received for his work as a joiner, he added a little to his income by playing the violin. There was a Jewish orchestra in the town that played for weddings, led by the tinsmith Moses Shakess, who took more than half of its earnings for himself. As Yakov played the fiddle extremely well, especially Russian songs, Shakess sometimes invited him to play in his orchestra for the sum of fifty kopeks a day, not including the presents he might receive from the guests. Whenever Bronze took his seat in the orchestra, the first thing that happened to him was that his face grew red, and the perspiration streamed from it, for the air was always hot, and reeking of garlic to the point of suffocation. Then his fiddle would begin to moan, and a double bass would croak hoarsely into his right ear, and a flute would weep into his left. This flute was played by a gaunt, red-bearded Jew with a network of red and blue veins on his face, who bore the name of a famous rich man, Rothschild. This confounded Jew always contrived to play even the merriest tunes sadly. For no obvious reason Yakov little by little began to conceive a feeling of hatred and contempt for all Jews, and especially for Rothschild. He quarrelled with him and abused him in ugly language, and once even tried to beat him, but Rothschild took offense at this, and cried with a fierce look:

"If I had not always respected you for your music, I should have thrown you out of the window long ago!"

Then he burst into tears. So after that Bronze was not often invited to play in the orchestra, and was only called upon in cases of dire necessity, when one of the Jews was missing.

Yakov was never in a good humor, because he always had to endure the most terrible losses. For instance, it was a sin to work on a Sunday or a holiday, and Monday was always a bad day, so in that way there were about two hundred days a year in which he was compelled to sit with his hands folded in his lap. That was a great loss to him. If anyone in town had a wedding without music, or if Shakess did not ask him to play, there was another loss. The police inspector had lain ill with consumption for two years while Yakov impatiently waited for him to die, and then had gone to take a cure in the city and had died there, which of course had meant another loss of at least ten rubles, as the coffin would have been an expensive one lined with brocade.

The thought of his losses worried Yakov at night more than at any other time, so he used to lay his fiddle at his side on the bed, and when those worries came trooping into his brain he would touch the strings, and the fiddle would give out a sound in the darkness, and Yakov's heart would feel lighter.

Last year on the sixth of May, Martha suddenly fell ill. The old woman breathed with difficulty, staggered in her walk, and felt terribly thirsty. Nevertheless, she got up that morning, lit the stove, and even went for the water. When evening came she went to bed. Yakov played his fiddle all day. When it grew quite dark, because he had nothing better to do, he took the book in which he kept an account of his losses, and began adding up the total for the year. They amounted to more than a thousand rubles. He was so shaken by this discovery that he threw the abacus to the floor and trampled in under foot. Then he picked it up again and rattled it once more for a long time, heaving as he did so sighs both deep and long. His face grew purple, and perspiration dripped from his brow. He was thinking that if those thousand rubles he had lost had been in the bank then, he would have had at least forty rubles interest by the end of the year. So those forty rubles were still another loss! In a word, wherever he turned he found losses and nothing but losses.

"Yakov!" cried Martha unexpectedly, "I am dying!"

He looked round at his wife. Her face was flushed with fever and looked unusually joyful and bright. Bronze was troubled, for he had been accustomed to seeing her pale and timid and unhappy. It seemed to him that she was already dead, and glad to have left this hut, and the coffins, and Yakov at last. She was staring at the ceiling, with her lips moving as if she saw her deliverer Death approaching and were whispering with him.

The dawn was just breaking and the eastern sky was glowing with a faint radiance. As he stared at the old woman, it somehow seemed to Yakov that he had never once spoken a tender word to her or pitied her; that he had never thought of buying her a kerchief or of bringing her back some sweets from a wedding. On the contrary, he had shouted at her and abused her for his losses, and had shaken his fist at her. It was true he had never beaten her, but he had frightened her no less, and she had been paralyzed with fear every time he had scolded her. Yes, and he had not allowed her to drink tea because his losses were heavy enough as it was, so she had had to be content with hot water. Now he understood why her face looked so strangely happy, and horror overwhelmed him.

As soon as it was light he borrowed a horse from a neighbor and took Martha to the hospital. As there were not many patients, he had not to wait very long – only about three hours. To his great satisfaction it was not the doctor who was receiving the sick that day, but his assistant, Maxim Nikolayich, an old man of whom it was said that although he quarreled and drank, he knew more than the doctor did.

"Good morning, Your Honor," said Yakov leading his old woman into the office. "Excuse us, Maxim Nikolayich, for intruding upon you with our trifling affairs. As you see, this subject has fallen ill. My life's friend, if you will allow me to use the expression – "

Knitting his gray eyebrows and stroking his whiskers, the doctor's assistant fixed his eyes on the old woman. She was sitting all in a heap on a low stool, and with her thin, long-nosed face and her open mouth, she looked like a thirsty bird.

"Hm, well-yes – " said the doctor slowly, heaving a sigh. "This is a case of influenza and possibly fever; there is typhoid in town. What's to be done? The old woman has lived a long life, thank God. How old is she?"

"She lacks one year of being seventy, Your Honor."

"Well, well, she has lived long. All things must come an end."

"You are certainly right, Maxim Nikolayich," said Yakov, smiling out of politeness. "And we thank you sincerely for your kindness, but allow me to suggest to you that even an insect dislikes to die!"

"Never mind if it does!" answered the doctor, as if the life or death of the old woman lay in his hands. "I'll tell you what you must do, my good man. Put a cold compress on her head, and give her two of these powders a day. Now then, good-bye! *Bonjour!*"

Yakov saw by the expression on the doctor's face that it was too late now for powders. He realized clearly that Martha would die very soon, if not today, then tomorrow. He touched the doctor's elbow gently, blinked, and whispered:

"She ought to be cupped, doctor!"

"I haven't time, I haven't time, my good man. Take your old woman and go, in God's name. Good-bye."

"Please, please, cup her, doctor!" begged Yakov. "You know yourself that if she had a pain in her stomach, powders and drops would do her good, but she has a cold! The first thing to do when one catches cold is to let some blood, Maxim Nikolayich!"

But the doctor had already sent for the next patient, and a woman leading a little boy came into the room.

"Go along, go along!" he cried to Yakov, frowning. "It's no use making a fuss!"

"Then at least put some leeches on her! I'll pray to God for you for the rest of my life!"

The doctor's temper flared up and he shouted:

"Don't say another word to me, blockhead!"

Yakov lost his temper, too, and flushed hotly, but he said nothing and, silently taking Martha's arm, led her out of the office. Only when they were once more seated in their wagon did he look fiercely and mockingly at the hospital and say:

"They're a pretty lot in there, they are! That doctor would have cupped a rich man, but he even begrudged a poor one a leech. Pigs!"

When they returned to the hut, Martha stood for nearly ten minutes supporting herself by the stove. She felt that if she lay down Yakov would begin to talk to her about his losses, and would scold her for lying down and not wanting to work. Yakov contemplated her sadly, thinking that tomorrow was St. John the Baptist's day, and the day after tomorrow was St. Nicholas the Wonder-Worker's day, and that the following day would be Sunday, and the day after that would be Monday, a bad day for work. So he would not be able to work for four days, and as Martha would probably die on one of these days, the coffin would have to be made at once. He took his iron yardstick in hand, went up to the old woman, and measured her. Then she lay down, and he crossed himself and went to work on the coffin.

When the task was completed Bronze put on his spectacles and wrote in his book:

"For 1 coffin for Martha Ivanov – 2 rubles, 40 kopeks."

He sighed. All day the old woman lay silent with closed eyes, but toward evening, when the daylight began to fade, she suddenly called the old man to her side.

"Do you remember, Yakov?" she asked. "Do you remember how fifty years ago God gave us a little baby with curly golden hair? Do you remember how you and I used to sit on the bank of the river and sing songs under the willow tree?" Then with a bitter smile she added: "The baby died."

Yakov racked his brains, but for the life of him he could not recall the child or the willow tree.

"You are dreaming," he said.

The priest came and administered the Sacrament and Extreme Unction. Then Martha began muttering unintelligibly, and toward morning she died.

The neighboring women washed her and dressed her, and laid her in her coffin. To avoid paying the deacon, Yakov read the psalms over her himself, and her grave cost him nothing, as the watchman of the cemetery was his cousin. Four peasants carried the coffin to the grave, not for money but for love. The old women, the beggars, and two village idiots followed the body, and the people whom they passed on the way crossed themselves devoutly. Yakov was very glad that everything had passed off so nicely and decently and cheaply, without giving offense to anyone. As he said farewell to Martha for the last time he touched the coffin with his hand and thought:

"That's a fine job!"

But walking homeward from the cemetery he was seized with great longing. He felt ill, his breath was burning hot, his legs grew weak, and he longed for a drink. Beside this, a thousand thoughts came crowding into his head. He remembered again that he had never once pitied Martha or said a tender word to her. The fifty years of their life together lay stretched far, far behind him, and somehow, during all that time, he had never once thought about her at all or noticed her more than if she had been a dog or a cat. And yet she had lit the stove every day, and had cooked and baked and fetched water and chopped wood, and when he had come home drunk from a wedding she had hung his fiddle reverently on a nail each time, and had silently put him to bed with a timid, anxious look on her face.

But here came Rothschild toward him, bowing and scraping and smiling.

"I have been looking for you, uncle!" he said. "Moses Shakess presents his compliments and wants you to go to him at once."

Yakov did not feel in a mood to do anything. He wanted to cry.

"Leave me alone!" he exclaimed, and walked on.

"Oh, how can you say that?" cried Rothschild, running beside him in alarm. "Moses will be very angry. He wants you to come at once!"

Yakov was disgusted by the panting of the Jew, by his blinking eyes, and by the quantities of reddish freckles on his face. He looked with aversion at his long green coat and at the whole of his frail, delicate figure.

"What do you mean by pestering me, garlic?" he shouted. "Get away!"

The Jew grew angry and shouted back:

"Don't yell at me like that or I'll send you flying over that fence!"

"Get out of my sight!" bellowed Yakov, shaking his fist at him. "There's no living in the same town with mangy curs like you!"

Rothschild was petrified with terror. He sank to the ground and waved his hands over his head as if to protect himself from falling blows; then he jumped up and ran away as fast as his legs could carry him. As he ran he leaped and waved his arms, and his long, gaunt back could be seen quivering. The little boys were delighted at what had happened, and ran after him screaming: "Jew, Jew!" The dogs also joined in the chase, barking. Somebody laughed and then whistled, at which the dogs barked louder and more vigorously still.

Then one of them must have bitten Rothschild, for a piteous, despairing scream rent the air.

Yakov walked across the common to the edge of the town without knowing where he was going, and the little boys shouted after him. "There goes old man Bronze! There goes old man Bronze!" He found himself by the river, where the snipe were darting about with shrill cries, and the ducks were quacking and swimming to and fro. The sun was shining fiercely and the water was sparkling so brightly that it was painful to look at. Yakov struck out onto a path that led along the riverbank. He came to a stout, red-checked woman just leaving a bathhouse. "Oh, you otter, you!" he thought. Not far from the bathhouse some little boys were fishing for crabs with pieces of meat. When they saw Yakov they shouted mischievously: "Old man Bronze! Old man Bronze!" But there before him stood an ancient, spreading willow tree with a massive trunk, and a crow's nest among its branches. Suddenly there flashed across Yakov's memory with all the vividness of life a little child with golden curls, and the willow of which Martha had spoken. Yes, this was the same tree, so green and peaceful and sad. How old it had grown, poor thing!

He sat down at its base and thought of the past. On the opposite shore, where that meadow now was, there had stood in those days a wood of tall birch trees, and that bare hill on the horizon yonder had been covered with the blue bloom of an ancient pine forest. And sailboats had plied the river then, but now all lay smooth and still, and only one little birch tree was left on the opposite bank, a graceful young thing, like a girl, while only ducks and geese plied the river. It was hard to believe that boats had once sailed here. It even seemed to him that there were fewer geese now than there had been. Yakov shut his eyes, and one by one white geese came flying toward him, an endless flock.

He was puzzled to know why he had never once been down to the river during the last forty or fifty years of his life, or, if he had been there, why he had never paid any attention to it. The stream was fine and large; he might have fished in it and sold the fish to the merchants and the government officials and the restaurant-keeper at the station, and put the money in the bank. He might have rowed in a boat from farm to farm and played on his fiddle. People of every rank would have paid money to hear him. He might have tried to run a boat on the river, that would have been better than making coffins. Finally, he might have raised geese, and killed them, and sent them to Moscow in the winter. Why, the down alone would have brought him ten rubles a year! But he had missed all these chances and had done nothing. What losses were here! Ah, what terrible losses! And, oh, if he had only done all these things at the same time! If he had only fished, and played the fiddle, and sailed a boat, and raised geese, what capital he would have had by now! But he had not even dreamed of doing all this; his life had gone by without profit or pleasure. It had been lost for nothing, not even a trifle. Nothing was left ahead; behind lay only losses, and such terrible losses that he shuddered to think of them. But why shouldn't men live so as to avoid all this waste and these losses? Why, oh why, should those birch and pine forests have been felled? Why should those meadows be lying so deserted? Why did people always do exactly what they ought not to do? Why had Yakov scolded and growled and clenched his fists and hurt his wife's feelings all his life? Why, oh why, had he frightened and insulted that Jew just now? Why did people in general always interfere with one another? What losses resulted from this! What terrible losses! If it were not for envy and anger they would get great profit from one another.

All that evening and night Yakov dreamed of the child, of the willow tree, of the fish and the geese, of Martha with her profile like a thirsty bird, and of Rothschild's pale, piteous mien. Queer faces seemed to be moving toward him from all sides, muttering to him about his losses. He tossed from side to side, and got up five times during the night to play his fiddle.

The next morning he rose with difficulty and walked to the hospital. The same doctor's assistant ordered him to put cold compresses on his head, and gave him little powders to take; by his expression and the tone of his voice Yakov knew that the state of affairs was bad, and that no powders could save him now. As he walked home he reflected that one good thing would result from his death: he would no longer have to eat and drink and pay taxes, neither would he offend people anymore, and, as a man lies in his grave for hundreds of thousands of years, the sum of his profits would be immense. So, life to a man was a loss – death, a gain. Of course this reasoning was correct, but it was also distressingly sad. Why should the world be so strangely arranged that a man's life, which was only given to him once, ought pass without profit?

He was not sorry then that he was going to die, but when he reached home, and saw his fiddle, his heart ached, and he regretted it deeply. He would not be able to take his fiddle with him into the grave, and now it would be left an orphan, and its fate would be that of the birch grove and the pine forest. Everything in the world had been lost, and would always be lost for ever. Yakov went out and sat on the threshold of his hut, clasping his fiddle to his breast. And as he thought of his life so full of waste and losses he began playing without knowing how piteous and touching his music was, and the tears streamed down his cheeks. And the more he thought the more sorrowfully his violin sang.

The latch clicked and Rothschild came in through the garden gate, walking boldly halfway across the garden. Then he suddenly stopped, crouched down, and, probably from fear, began making signs with his hands as if he were trying to show on his fingers what time it was.

"Come on, don't be afraid!" said Yakov gently, beckoning him to advance. "Come on!"

With many mistrustful and fearful glances, Rothschild went slowly up to Yakov, and stopped about two yards away.

"Please don't beat me!" he said with a ducking bow. "Moses Shakess has sent me to you again. 'Don't be afraid,' he said, 'go to Yakov,' says he, 'and say that we can't possibly manage without him.' There is a wedding next Thursday. Ye-es sir. Mr. Shapovalov is marrying his daughter to a very fine man. It will be an expensive wedding, ai, ai!" added the Jew with a wink.

"I can't go" said Yakov breathing hard. "I'm ill, brother."

And he began to play again, and the tears gushed out of his eyes over his fiddle. Rothschild listened intently with his head turned away and his arms folded on his breast. The startled, irresolute look on his face gradually gave way to one of suffering and grief. He cast up his eyes as if in an ecstasy of agony and murmured: "Okh-okh!" And the tears began to trickle slowly down his cheeks, and to drip over his green coat.

All day Yakov lay and suffered. When the priest came in the evening to administer the Sacrament he asked him if he could not think of any particular sin.

Struggling with his fading memories, Yakov recalled once more Martha's sad face, and the despairing cry of the Jew when the dog had bitten him. He murmured almost inaudibly:

"Give my fiddle to Rothschild."

"It shall be done," answered the priest.

So it happened that everyone in the little town began asking:

"Where did Rothschild get that good fiddle? Did he buy it or steal it or get it from a pawnshop?"

Rothschild has long since abandoned his flute, and now only plays on the violin. The same mournful notes flow from his bow that used to come from his flute, and when he tries to repeat what Yakov played as he sat on the threshold of his hut, the result is an air so plaintive and sad that everyone who hears him weeps, and he himself at last raises his eyes and murmurs: "Okh-okh!" And this new song has so delighted the town that the merchants and government officials vie with each other in getting Rothschild to come to their houses, and sometimes make him play it ten times in succession.

First published in Russian: 1894
Translation by Marian Fell

Eighteenth century woodcut of a Sami shaman.

With his early stories and novels, Pelevin established himself as one of Russia's leading contemporary writers. "The Tambourine of the Upper World" showcases many of his usual themes and interests: social satire, mysticism, metaphysical border crossings, and upturned expectations.

The Tambourine of the Upper World
Victor Pelevin

As he stepped into the carriage, the policeman glanced in passing at Tanya and Masha before looking over at the corner – then he stopped in his tracks and stared in astonishment at the woman sitting there.

The woman really did look very odd. Her Mongoloid face, which resembled a three-day-old pancake curling up at the edges, offered absolutely no indication of her age, especially as her eyes were concealed by ribbons of leather and strings of beads. Although the weather was warm, she was wearing a fur hat with three wide leather bands – one of them ran round her forehead to the back of her head, and hanging down from it over her face, shoulders and chest were leather braids tied with little bronze figures, bells and other charms. The other two leather bands criss-crossed over the top of her head, where a crudely cast metal bird perched, stretching its long twisted neck up to the sky.

The woman was dressed in a long broad homespun shirt with thin strips of reindeer fur, decorated with leather braiding, small gleaming plates of metal and little bells which made a rather pleasant melodic sound at every jolt of the train. There were numerous small items of obscure significance fastened to her shirt – zig-zag iron arrows, two Medals of Honor, tin faces stamped without mouths and on her right shoulder, hanging from a Cross of St. George ribbon there were two long rusty nails. The woman was clutching an elongated leather tambourine, also decorated with numerous little bells; the rim of another tambourine protruded from the capacious sports bag on which she was squatting.

"Documents," said the policeman at last. The woman made no response at all.

"She's travelling with me," Tanya put in, "and she hasn't got any documents. And she doesn't understand Russian."

Tanya spoke in the weary voice of someone who has to explain the same thing again and again, several times a day.

"How's that, no documents?"

"Why should an elderly woman carry documents around with her? All her papers are in Moscow, in the Ministry of Culture. She's here with a folk-music and dance group."

"Why's she dressed up like that?" asked the policeman.

"National costume," Tanya answered. "She's an Honored Reindeer-Herder. She has medals for it, see, there, to the right of that bell."

"We're not in the tundra here. It's a breach of social order."

"What order?" said Tanya, raising her voice. "Just what kind of order are you trying to defend? The puddles in the compartments? Or the stench of that lot?" She nodded towards the partition, behind which drunken shouting could be heard. "Instead of keeping them under control, all you can do is check an old woman's documents."

The policeman looked doubtfully at the woman Tanya had called old. She sat there quietly in the corner, swaying in time with the train, not paying the least attention to the argument being conducted about her. Despite her strange appearance, her small figure radiated such a calm and peaceful energy that when the lieutenant had looked at her for a minute or so he relented: he seemed to smile at something very far away, and his left fist ceased its mechanical chafing of the truncheon hanging at his belt.

"What's her name?" he asked.

"Tyimy," Tanya replied. "All right," said the policeman sliding the heavy door of the carriage aside. "But just be careful..."

The door closed behind him and the howls from beyond the partition became a little quieter. The train braked and for a few damp seconds the young women found themselves facing a bumpy asphalt platform, and beyond it low buildings with numerous chimneys of all heights and diameters, some smoking feebly.

"Krematovo station," the loudspeaker announced with a passionless female voice, when the doors had already slammed shut, "Next station – Forty-Third Mile."

"Is that ours?" Tanya asked.

Masha nodded and looked at Tyimy, who was still sitting impassively in the corner. "Has she been with you for long?"

"More than two years now," Tanya answered.

"Is she hard to get along with?"

"Oh, no," said Tanya, "she's very quiet. She sits in the kitchen just like that all the time. Watches television."

"Doesn't she ever go out for a walk?"

"No," said Tanya, "she doesn't go out. She sleeps on the balcony sometimes."

"Doesn't she find it hard? Living in the city, I mean?"

"It was hard for her at first," said Tanya, "then she got used to it. At first she used to bang her tambourine all night long and wrestle with someone invisible. There are lots of spirits in the center. Now it seems they're all her servants. She hung those two nails on her shoulder, see? She defeated them all. But she still hides in the bathroom when there's a firework display."

The Forty-Third Mile station was well suited to its name. Close to a railway station there is usually some kind of human settlement, but here there was nothing except the brick hut of the ticket office, and the only idea with which the place could possibly be associated was its distance from Moscow. The forest began immediately beyond the barrier, and it stretched out as far as the eye could see – it was a mystery where the few ragged passengers waiting for the train could have come from. Masha went ahead, bowed down under the weight of her bag. Tanya walked beside her, carrying a similar bag on her shoulder, and Tyimy brought up the rear, her bells jangling, lifting up the hem of her skirt when she had to stride across a puddle.

She was wearing blue Chinese sports shoes and her calves were clad in broad leather leggings embroidered with fine beads. Masha looked round several times, and she noticed that Tyimy had the round dial of an alarm clock sewn to her left legging and a horseshoe fastened to her right legging with a lavatory chain, so that it almost trailed in the mud.

"Listen, Tanya," she asked quietly, "what's she got that horseshoe for?"

"For the Lower World," said Tanya. "Everything there's covered in mud. That's so she won't get stuck."

Masha was going to ask her about the clock-face, but she decided not to.

A fine paved road led away from the station into the forest, with old birch trees ranged evenly along both sides, but three or four hundred yards further on all order in the distribution of the trees had disappeared, and then the asphalt imperceptibly petered out and they found themselves slopping through wet mud that sucked at their feet.

Masha thought that once upon a time there must have been a big boss who gave orders for an asphalt road to be laid through the forest, but then since it turned out it wasn't going anywhere in particular, the road was abandoned and forgotten. The sight of it made Masha sad, and her own life, begun some twenty-five years ago through some unknown act of will, suddenly seemed like another road of the same kind: straight and even at first, running between neat, even rows of simple truths, and then – forgotten by some unknown boss – transformed into a crooked track leading God knows where.

Up ahead she caught a glimpse of a piece of white braided cloth tied to a branch of a birch tree.

"Here," said" Masha, "we turn right into the forest. About another five hundred yards."

"That's very close," Tanya said doubtfully, "how could it possibly have survived?"

"No one ever comes here," Masha answered. "There's nothing there, and half the forest is fenced off with barbed wire."

Soon the first low concrete pillar appeared ahead of them, with drooping barbed wire leading off both sides. Then a few more pillars came into sight, older land overgrown with dense bushes, so that the barbed wire was invisible until they came really close. The girls walked in silence along the fence until Masha halted at another piece of white braid dangling from a bush.

"Here," she said.

Several strands of the barbed wire had been pulled up and tangled over each other. Masha and Tanya ducked under it without any difficulty, but for some reason Tyimy went through backwards, snagging her shirt. She spent a long time squirming in the gap with her bells jangling.

Beyond the wire the forest was exactly the same; there were no signs at all of human activity. Masha moved ahead confidently, halting after a few minutes at the edge of a ravine with a small stream babbling at its bottom.

"We're here," she said, "it's over there in those bushes."

Tanya looked down. "I can't see anything."

"That's the tail sticking up over there," said Masha, pointing, "and there's the wing. Come on, there's a way down over here."

Tyimy didn't go down, but sat on Tanya's bag, leaned back against a tree and became perfectly still. Masha and Tanya went down into the ravine, clutching at branches and slipping over the wet earth. .

"Tell me, Tanya," Masha said in a quiet voice, "doesn't she need to take a look? How will she manage?"

"Don't worry about that," said Tanya, gazing off into the bushes, "she knows better than we – she really does. How on earth could this have been preserved?"

Behind the bushes there was something colored a dark dirty brown, extremely old. At first glance it resembled the burial site of a minor nomadic prince who at the very last moment had accepted some strange form of Christianity. A broad cross-shaped twisted metal structure protruded crookedly from a long narrow mound of earth. With an effort it was recognizable as the badly-damaged tail of an airplane that had broken away from the fuselage on impact. The fuselage had almost completely sunk into the ground: a few yards ahead of them they could make out among the hazel bushes and the grass the contours of the broken wings, and see a cross on one of them where the dirt had been rubbed away.

"I looked it up in a book," said Masha, breaking the silence, "apparently it's an assault aircraft, a Heinkel. There were two different models, one had a canon under the fuselage and the other had something else, I don't remember what. Anyway, it's not important."

"Did you open the cockpit?" Tanya asked.

"No," said Masha, "I was too scared to on my own."

"What if there's nobody there?"

"There must be," said Masha, "the glass is intact. Take a look." She stepped forward, pushed aside a few branches and with the edge of her hand scraped away a layer of humus that had taken years to form.

Tanya bent her face down close to the glass. Beyond it she could see something dark-colored that seemed to be wet.

"How many of them were there?" she asked. "If this is a Heinkel, then surely there should be a gunner too?"

"I don't know," said Masha.

"All right," said Tanya, "Tyimy will find out. It's a pity the cockpit's closed. If we just had a clump of hair or a bone it would make things much easier."

"Can't she manage with this?"

"Yes, she can," said Tanya, "only it takes longer. It's starting to get dark already. Let's go and collect branches."

"But won't it affect the quality?"

"Quality?" Tanya asked. "What could quality possibly mean in this business?"

The fire was blazing up well and already giving more light than the evening sky covered by low clouds. Masha noticed that she now had a long shadow dancing impatiently across the grass; it upset her that the shadow was clearly so much more confident than she was. Masha felt stupid in her city clothes, but in the flickering firelight Tyimy's costume, which everyone they had met during the day had stared at in wide-eyed astonishment, now seemed like the most comfortable and natural clothing a person could possibly wear.

"Well then," said Tanya, "we'll get started soon."

"What are we waiting for?" Masha asked in a whisper.

"Don't be in such a hurry," Tanya answered just as quietly, "she knows when everything has to be done. Don't say anything to her right now."

Masha sat down on the ground beside her friend. "It's terrifying," she said, running her hand over the spot on her jacket behind which her heart lay. "How long do we wait?"

"I don't know; it's always different. Last year there…"

Masha shuddered. The dry note of the tambourines rang out above the meadow, followed by the jangling of many small bells.

Tyimy was standing up, leaning forward and staring into the bushes at the edge of the ravine. She struck the tambourine again, ran anti-clockwise twice round the clearing, leapt the wall of bushes with incredible ease and vanished into the ravine. From down below came a pitiful shout filled with pain, and Masha was sure Tyimy must have broken her leg, but Tanya merely closed her eyes reassuringly.

They heard quick blows on the tambourine and rapidly mumbled words. Then everything went quiet and Tyimy emerged from the bushes. Her movements now were slow and ceremonial. When she reached the center of the clearing she stopped, lifted up her hands and began beating rhythmically on the tambourine. Just to be on the safe side Masha closed her eyes.

Soon a new sound was added to the beating of the tambourine. Masha didn't notice when it actually began and at first she couldn't understand what it was: it seemed as though some unfamiliar string instrument was playing close by, and then she realized that the piercing hollow note was produced by Tyimy's voice.

The sound of the voice seemed to exist in some absolutely separate space, a space which it created and then moved through, running in its course into many objects of an uncertain nature, each of which drew from Tyimy several harsh guttural sounds. For some reason Masha imagined a net dredging across the bottom of a dark pool, gathering in everything in its path. Suddenly Tyimy's voice snagged on something and Masha could feel her struggling ineffectively to break free.

Masha opened her eyes. Tyimy was standing quite close to the fire and trying to pull back her wrist out of empty space. She was jerking back her arm with all her strength, but the emptiness would not loosen its grip.

"Nilti dolgong," Tyimy said threateningly, *"nilti djamai!"*

Masha had the distinct feeling that the void facing Tyimy said something in reply.

Tyimy laughed and shook her tambourine.

"Nein, Herr General!" she said *"Da hat mit Ihnen gar nicht zu tun. Ich bin hier wegen ganz anderer Angelegenheit."*

The void asked something and Tyimy shook her head.

"Does she speak German, then?" Masha asked.

"When she's in contact she does," said Tanya. "She can speak any language then."

Tyimy made another attempt to pull her hand free. *"Heute ist schon zu spät, Herr General. Verzeirheng, ich hab es sehr eilig,"* she shouted in exasperation.

This time Masha could feel the threat from the void.

"Wozu?" Tyimy shouted derisively, then tore the Cross of St. George ribbon with the two rusty nails off her shoulder and swung it above her head. *"Nilti djamai! Blyai budulan!"*

The void released her hand so suddenly that Tyimy fell back into the grass. On the ground she started to laugh, then turned to Tanya and Masha and shook her head.

"What's happened?" Masha asked. "Bad news, I'm afraid," said Tanya. "Your client's not in the Lower World."

"Perhaps she didn't look everywhere?" Masha suggested.

''What everywhere? There isn't any *where* down there. No beginning to it, and no end."

"So what do we do now?"

"We can try looking in the Upper World," said Tanya. "There's not much chance, it's never worked before. But that's no reason not to try." She turned to Tyimy where she was still sitting on the grass and pointed upwards. Tyimy nodded, went over to her bag and took out the other tambourine. Then she reached for a can of Coca-Cola, shook her head and took a few gulps. Masha was reminded of Martina Navratilova on the center court at Wimbledon.

The Tambourine of the Upper World had a different sound, quieter and more thoughtful. Tyimy's voice was different too, picking out a long mournful note. Instead of fear Masha felt reconciliation and a gentle sadness. The events of a few minutes before were repeated, but this time it was not terrible, it was exalted – and inappropriate. Inappropriate because even Masha realized that there was absolutely no point in disturbing the regions of the world that Tyimy was now addressing with her face turned up to the sky, while she tapped lightly on her tambourine.

Masha recalled an old cartoon about a small grey wolf wandering around in the narrow, confined spaces of suburban Moscow, with their daubed, depressing colors. In the animated film, all of this sometimes disappeared and out of nowhere would appear an open expanse drenched in midday sunlight, an almost transparent space, with a lightly sketched figure wandering along a pale watercolor road.

Masha shook her head to clear her mind and then looked around. All the components of her surroundings, all these bushes and trees, the grass and plants and the sky, which only a moment ago had been in direct contact with each other, seemed to have been shaken loose by the music of the tambourine. For a moment a strange, bright, unfamiliar world peeped out through the cracks between them.

Tyimy's voice snagged against something, tried to move on and couldn't. It stuck on a single taut note.

Tanya tugged at Masha's sleeve.

"Look, he's there," she said, "We've found him. Now she'll hook him…"

Tyimy raised up her arms, gave a piercing cry and tumbled over into the grass.

Masha heard a plane rumbling in the distance. Though the sound went on and on, she couldn't make out where it was coming from, and when it stopped she heard a whole series of noises: a blow on glass; a clanging of rusty iron; the quiet but distinct sound of a man coughing.

Tanya got up and took a few steps towards the ravine. Masha noticed a dark figure standing at the edge of the clearing.

"Sprechen Sie Deutsch?" Tanya asked in a hoarse voice.

The figure moved silently towards the fire.

"Sprechen Sie Deutsch?" Tanya repeated, backing away. "Is he deaf or something?"

The red glow of the fire revealed a stocky man of about forty in a leather jacket and a flying-helmet. Moving closer, he sat down opposite the giggling Tyimy, crossed his legs and looked up at Tanya.

"Sprechen Sie Deutsch?"

"Stop saying that, will you," the man replied quietly in Russian, "the same thing over and over."

Tanya whistled in disappointment. "Who are you, then?" she asked.

"Me? Major Zvyagintsev. Nikolai Ivanovich Zvyagintsev. And just who are you?"

Masha and Tanya exchanged glances.

"I don't understand," said Tanya. "What's a Major Zvyagintsev doing in a German plane?"

"A captured plane," said the major. "I was moving it to another aerodrome and then..."

Major Zvyagintsev's face contorted, and they could see he'd remembered something extremely unpleasant.

"You mean to say," asked Tanya, "you're a Soviet flyer?"

"I don't know about that," answered Major Zvyagintsev. "I used to be, but now I'm not sure. Everything's different where I am now."

He looked up at Masha; she looked away, embarrassed.

"What are you doing here, girls?" he asked. "The paths of the living and the dead never cross. Isn't that so?"

"Oh," said Tanya, "please, we're sorry. We never disturb Soviet flyers. It's all because of the plane. We thought there was a German in it."

"And what do you want with a German?"

Masha raised her eyes and looked at the major. He had a broad face with a calm expression, a slightly turned-up nose and several days' stubble on his cheeks. Masha liked faces like that. The major's appearance was a little spoiled by the bullet hole in his left temple, but Masha had long ago come to the conclusion that there is no such thing as perfection in this world, and she didn't look for it in people – especially not in the way they looked.

"It's the times we live in now," said Tanya, "everyone has to earn a crust as best they can. My friend and me..."

She nodded towards the impassive Tyimy.

"Well, let's just say, it's our job. Everybody's leaving nowadays. Marrying a foreigner costs four thousand in dollars, and we fix it for about five hundred."

"You mean dead men?" the major asked incredulously.

"What of it? They still have their citizenship. We bring them back to life on condition that they get married. Usually they're Germans. A German corpse is worth about the same as a live black man from Zimbabwe or a Russian-speaking Jew without a visa. The best catch of all, of course, is a

Spaniard from the Blue Division, but that's an expensive kind of corpse. Very rare. There are Italians as well, and Finns. But we don't touch Romanians or Hungarians."

"So that's it," said the major. "And do they live very long afterwards?"'

"About three years," said Tanya.

"Not very long. Don't you feel sorry for them?"

Tanya thought for a moment. Her beautiful face became quite serious and a deep fold appeared between her eyebrows. The only sound in the silence was the crackling of twigs in the fire and the quiet rustling of leaves.

"That's straight to the point," she said eventually. "Do you seriously want to know?"

"Absolutely."

Tanya thought for a little longer. "What I've heard," she began, "is that there's a law of earth and a law of heaven. If you can manifest heavenly power on earth, then all the creatures in being are set in motion and the invisible will be made visible. They have no inner substance – they only consist of a temporary condensation of darkness. That's why, in this constant cycle of transformations, they don't last for long. And since their essence is nothing but void, I don't feel sorry for them."

"That's precisely right," said the major, "you understand it very well."

The furrow between Tanya's brows relaxed.

"To be honest, most of the time there's so much work that I don't have time to think about it. We usually do about ten a month, less in winter. In Moscow, Tyimy's booked-up in advance for two years."

"And what about the men you bring back to life, do they always agree?"

"Almost always," said Tanya. "It's so terribly dreary there. Dark and crowded, nothing heavenly. The gnashing of teeth. I don't know what it's like where you are, we haven't had any clients from the Upper World. But even down below, of course, the dead are all different. A year ago we had a really terrible case down near Kharkov. Got stuck with this tank driver from the Death's Head Division. We dressed him, washed him, shaved him, explained everything. He said he agreed. His bride was lovely, Marina her name was, from Moscow University. I think she got fixed up with a Japanese sailor afterwards – God, you should see the way they come floating up out of the sea, whenever I think about it... What was I talking about?"

"The tank-driver," said the major.

"Oh, yes. Well, to keep it short, we gave him a little money to make him feel at home. So of course he started drinking, they all drink at first. And then in some kiosk they refused to sell him vodka. They wanted rubles, and all he had was coupons and occupation deutschmarks. First he blew away their window with his gun, then he drove in that night on his Tiger and flattened all the kiosks in front of the railway station. Ever since then people keep seeing that tank at night. He drives around Kharkov flattening kiosks. In the daytime he just disappears. No one knows where."

"Strange things like that happen," said the major, "the world is a strange place."

"Ever since then we only work with the Wehrmacht. We won't have anything to do with the SS. They're all out of their skulls. And they don't want to get married, their code won't allow it."

A strong gust of cold wind blew across the clearing. Masha tore her fascinated gaze away from the face of Major Zvyagintsev and saw three shadowy transparent figures emerge from behind a tree standing at the edge of the clearing. Tyimy screeched in fright and instantly hid behind Tanya.

"Here we go," mumbled Tanya. "We're off again. Don't be so afraid of them, you old biddy, they won't touch you."

She stood up and went towards the transparent figures, gesturing reassuringly to them from a distance, just like a driver who has broken the law waves to the policeman who has pulled him over. Tyimy huddled up in a tight ball, pressed her head against her knees and trembled like a leaf. Just to be on the safe side Masha moved closer to the fire and suddenly she felt the full force of Major Zvyagintsev's gaze. She raised her eyes. The major smiled sadly.

"You're beautiful, Masha," he said quietly. "When your Tyimy began to call me, I was working in the garden. She called and called until I was really annoyed.I wanted to scare you all away, so I glanced out, and then I saw you, Masha. I was dumbfounded, I don't have the words to express it. In school I had a friend who looked like you – Varya her name was. She was just like you, with the same freckles on her nose. If not for you, Masha, why would I have bothered to come here?"

"You have a garden there?" Masha asked, blushing slightly.

"Yes."

"And what's the place where you live called?"

""We don't have any names," said the major, "and so we live in peace and joy."

"But what's it like there?"

"Fine," said the major, and he smiled again.

"Well, do you have things, like people do?"

"How can I explain, Masha? We do, but then we don't. Everything's a bit indefinite, a bit vague. But that's only if you start thinking about it."

"Where do you live?"

"I have something like a little house and a plot of land. It's quiet there, very nice."

"Do you have a car?" Masha asked, and then felt embarrassed because her question seemed so stupid.

"If I want one, it's there. Why shouldn't it be?"

"What kind?"

"It varies," said the major. "And sometimes I have a microwave oven, and what's it called... a washing machine. Only there's nothing to wash. And sometimes I have a color television. There's only one channel, but it has all of yours in it."

"Is it a different kind of television every time, too?"

"Yes," said the major."Sometimes it's a Panasonic, sometimes a Shivaki. But when you look very closely, it's gone, nothing but mist hanging in the air... It's like I said, everything's just like it is here, only there aren't any names. Everything is nameless. And the higher you go, the more nameless everything becomes."

Masha couldn't think of any more questions to ask, so she said nothing and pondered the major's last words. Meanwhile Tanya was passionately trying to convince the three transparent, formless figures about something.

"I told you already, she's working charms against the thunder," they heard her say. "It's all perfectly legal. When she was a child she was struck by lightning and then the thunder-god gave her a piece of tin so she could make herself a visor... What am I supposed to show you? Why should she carry that kind of thing around with her? We've never had this kind of problem before... You should be ashamed of yourselves pestering an old woman. You'd be better off sorting out those folk-healers in Moscow. That rotten filth, it's enough to scare you to death, and you come here bothering an old woman...I'm going to put in a complaint..."

Masha felt the major touch her elbow. "Masha," he said, "I'm going now. I want to leave you something to remember me by."

Masha liked the familiar tone of voice he was using with her now.

"What is it?" she asked.

"A pipe," said the major. "A reed pipe. Whenever you grow weary of this life, come here to my airplane. If you play, I'll come to you."

"And will I be able to visit your home?" Masha asked.

"Yes," said the major. "You'll eat strawberries. You should see the strawberries I have there."

He stood up.

"Will you come?" he asked. "I'll be waiting."

Masha nodded almost imperceptibly.

"But how can you? You're alive now..."

The major shrugged, took a rusty TT revolver out of his leather jacket and set the barrel to his ear.

The shot was like thunder.

Tanya turned-round and stared in horror at the major, who swayed, but remained standing on his feet. Tyimy raised her head and began giggling. There was another gust of cold wind, and Masha saw that the transparent figures were gone from the edge of the clearing.

"I'll be waiting," Major Zvyagintsev repeated and, swaying slightly, he walked over to the ravine, where a faint rainbow radiance hung in the air. A few more steps and his figure dissolved in the darkness, like a lump of sugar in a glass of hot tea.

Masha looked out through the train window at the vegetable gardens and little houses rushing past and wept quietly.

"What's wrong Masha, what is it?" said Tanya, looking into her tear-stained face. "Forget it – it happens sometimes. Why don't you come up to Arkhangelsk with the other girls? There's a B-29 in the swamp there, an American Flying Fortress. Eleven men, enough for everybody. Will you come?"

"When did you want to go?" asked Masha. "Sometime after the fifteenth. You should come round on the fifteenth anyway, for the Festival of the Clean Tent. Say you'll come. Tyimy's already dried the toadstools. We'll play the Tambourine of the Upper World, since you liked it so much. Tyimy, wouldn't it be great if Masha came round?"

Tyimy lifted up her face and gave a broad smile in reply, revealing brown stumps of teeth protruding in various directions from her gums. The smile looked terrifying because her eyes were concealed by the leather ribbons dangling from her hat – it seemed as though only her mouth was smiling and that the expression in her invisible eyes would be cold and curious.

"Don't be afraid," said Tanya, "she's very kind, really."

But Masha was already looking out of the window. In her pocket her fingers were clutching the reed pipe that Major Zvyagintsev had given her, and she was thinking very hard.

First published in Russian: 1991
Translation by Andrew Bromfield

Не пой, красавица, при мне
Александр Пушкин

Не пой, красавица, при мне
Ты песен Грузии печальной:
Напоминают мне оне
Другую жизнь и берег дальный.

Увы! напоминают мне
Твои жестокие напевы
И степь, и ночь – и при луне
Черты далёкой, бедной девы.

Я призрак милый, роковой,
Тебя увидев, забываю;
Но ты поёшь – и предо мной
Его я вновь воображаю.

Не пой, красавица, при мне
Ты песен Грузии печальной:
Напоминают мне оне
Другую жизнь и берег дальный.

My Beauty, Do Not Sing to Me
Alexander Pushkin

My beauty, do not sing to me
Your songs of Georgia melancholy.
They call to mind too vividly
That distant life of youthful folly.

Alas, those ruthless melodies,
For me with moonlit steppe are laden
And most of all with memories:
The face of that poor, distant maiden.

Your beauty nearly had replaced
That sweet portentous apparition;
But then your songs recalled that place,
And once again I see that vision.

My beauty, do not sing to me
Your songs of Georgia melancholy.
They call to mind too vividly
That distant life of youthful folly.

First published in Russian: 1828
Translation by Lydia Razran Stone

Portrait of A.N. Scriabin
Alexander Golovin (1915)

Before committing himself to poetry, Pasternak considered pursuing a career in music. In these early chapters from his memoir he recounts his early fascination with music and his relationship with the composer Alexander Scriabin.

Safe Conduct
Boris Pasternak

II

Three years went by and it was winter out of doors. The street was fore-shortened by at least a third with twilight and with furs. The cubes of carriages and lanterns sped along it silently. An end was put to the inheritance of conventions interrupted even before this more than once. They were washed away by the wave of a more powerful right to succession – that of personalities.

I shall not describe in detail what preceded this. How in a mode of feeling, reminiscent of Gumilov's "sixth-sense," nature was revealed to a ten-year-old. How botany appeared as his first passion in response to the five-petalled persistence of the plant. How names, sought out according to the classified text, brought peace to eyes of flowers that seemed filled with scent, in their unquestioning rush towards Linnaeus, as if from nonentity to fame.

How in the spring of 1901 a troop of Dahomeyan Amazons was on show at the Zoological Gardens. How for me the first sensation of woman was bound up with the sensation of a naked band, of closed ranks of misery, a tropical parade to the sound of a drum. How I became a slave to forms, earlier than one should, because I saw in these women the form of slaves too soon. How in the summer of 1903 in Obelenski where the Scriabins lived next door to us, the ward of friends of ours who lived beyond the Prot, was nearly drowned. How the student who rushed to her aid met his death, and subsequently she herself went mad after several attempts at suicide from the same steep place. How later, when I broke my leg, in one evening ensuring my absence from two future wars, and was lying motionless in plaster of paris, the house of these friends over the river caught fire and the shrill village fire alarm, shaking feverishly, rang like mad. How, taut like a kite in the sky, the jagged conflagration beat upon the air, and suddenly, wrenching the splintering latticework away with the chimney, dived head over heels into the layer of purple grey smoke. How my father's hair turned grey at the sight of the circling glare which reared in a cloud above the forest road from two miles off, as he galloped with the doctor that night from Maloyaroslavitz, and was filled with the conviction that this was the woman dear to him, being burnt with three children, and with a 100-lb. weight on the plaster of paris, which she could not possibly lift without running the risk of crippling the leg for life.

I shall not describe this, my reader will do that for me. He likes fables and horrors and looks upon history as upon a tale which is continued without end. It is impossible to tell whether he wishes the tale to have a reasonable conclusion. He likes those places best beyond which his walks have never extended. He is submerged in prefaces and introductions but life opens for me only in the place where he is inclined to balance accounts. Not to mention the fact that the inner parts of history are stamped on my understanding in the image of impending death, in life too, I lived wholly only on those occasions when the wearisome preparation of parts was over, and having dined off the finished dish, a complete feeling burst into freedom with the whole extent of space before it.

And so, it was winter out of doors, the street was foreshortened by at least a third with twilight, and the whole day was in a rush. Falling behind the street in the whirlwind of snowflakes the lanterns raced in their own whirlwind. On the way from school the name Scriabin, all in snow, tumbled from the concert bill on to my back. I brought it home with me on the lid of my school-satchel, water trickled from it onto the window sill. This adoration struck me more cruelly and no less fantastically than a fever. On seeing him, I would turn pale, only to flush deeply immediately afterwards for this very pallor. If he spoke to me my wits deserted me and amid the general laughter I would hear myself answering something that was not to the point, but what exactly – I could never hear. I knew that he guessed everything but had not once come to my aid. This meant that he did not pity me, and this was just that unanswerable indivisible feeling for which I thirsted. This feeling alone, the more fiery it was, the more it protected me from the desolation which his incommunicable music inspired.

Before his departure for Italy he came to take his leave of us. He played – that one cannot describe – he had supper with us, he started philosophizing, became ingenuous, joked. I kept feeling that he was inwardly very bored. They started saying good-bye. Good wishes re-echoed. Into the general heap of parting benedictions fell mine like a clot of blood. All this was said on the move and the exclamations crowding in doorways gradually descended to the hall. There everything was repeated with a resumed impetuosity and with the hook of his collar, which would not slip into the tightly sewn loop for a long time. The door banged, the key turned twice. Walking past the piano, which still spoke of his playing with the whole fretted lighting of the music stand, my mother sat down to glance through the *etudes* he had left, and only the first sixteen bars of the prelude had fallen together, full of some surprised preparedness, not to be rewarded by anything on earth, when I rolled downstairs and without a coat or hat, ran along the dark Myasnitskaya to make him come back or see him just once again.

This has been experienced by everyone. Tradition has appeared to us all, it has promised us all a face, and it has fulfilled its promise to us all in different ways. We have all become people according to the measure in which we have loved people and have had occasion for loving. Tradition, hiding behind the nickname of the medium in which one finds oneself, has never been satisfied with the compound image invented about it, but has always sent us someone of its most decisive exceptions. Why, then, has the majority passed away in the guise of a blurred generality, barely tolerable and bearable? It has preferred the faceless to faces, frightened by the sacrifices which tradition demands of childhood. To love selflessly and unconditionally, with a strength equal to the square root of distance is the task of our hearts while we are children.

III

Of course I did not catch up to him, but very likely I did not even think of that. We met again after six years on his return from abroad. This date fell full upon my adolescent years. And everyone knows how boundless adolescence is. However many decades accrue to us afterwards, they are powerless to fill that hangar, into which they fly for memories, separately and in crowds, day and night, like learner aeroplanes for petrol. In other words, these years in our life form a part which excels the whole, and Faust, who lived through them twice, lived through the absolutely unimaginable, which can be measured only by the mathematical paradox.

Scriabin arrived and the rehearsals for "Extase" began immediately. How I would like now to change this title, which smells of a tightly wrapped soap carton, for one more suitable! The rehearsals took place in the mornings. The way there lay through melting gloom, along Furkasovsky and Kuznetsky, which lay submerged in icy bread in *kvass*. Along the somnolent streets the hanging tongues of the belfries sank into the mist. In each a solitary bell clanged once. The rest remained in friendly silence together, with the full restraint of fasting metal. Nikitskaya Street beat egg in cognac at the end of Gazetnoy Street in the echoing abyss of the crossroads. Noisily the forged sledge-runners rode into the puddles and the flintstone tapped under the walking-sticks of the members of the orchestra.

The concert hall resembled a circus during the hours of the morning cleaning. The cages of the amphitheater gaped empty. Slowly the stalls filled. Driven against its will in the sticks into the winter half, the music slapped its paw from there upon the wooden front of the organ. Suddenly the public would begin to appear in an even stream, as though the town were being cleared for the enemy. The music was let loose. Many-hued, breaking into infinite fragments, multiplying itself lightning flash on flash, it leapt the platform and was scattered there. It was tuned up, it raced with a feverish haste towards harmony and suddenly reaching the pitch of an un-heard-of blending, broke off at the very height of its deep sounding whirl-wind, dying away and straightening up along the footlights.

It was man's first settlement in the worlds, revealed by Wagner for fictive beings and mastodons. In one place a lyrical dwelling not fictitious arose, materially equal to the whole universe which had been ground down for its bricks. Above the fence of the symphony burned Van Gogh's sun. Its window-sills were covered with Chopin's dusty archives. The inmates did not poke their noses into this dust, but actualized the best testaments of their forefathers in all their arrangements.

I could not hear this music without tears. It was engraved on my mem-ory before it lay on the zincographic plates of the first proofs. There was nothing unexpected in this. The hand which wrote it had been laid upon me six years back with no less weight.

What had all these years been but the succeeding transformation of the living imprint, given up to the will of growth? It was not surprising that in this symphony I met an enviably fortunate contemporary. Its proximity could not fail to be reflected on people near it, on my occupations, on my whole way of life. And this is how it was reflected.

I loved music more than anything else, and I loved Scriabin more than anyone else in the world of music. I began to lisp in music not long before my first acquaintance with him. On his return I was the pupil of a composer even now alive and well. I had only to go through orchestration. All sorts of things were said, but the only important thing is that even if only antag-onistic things had been said I could not imagine a life not lived in music.

But I did not possess absolute pitch. That is the name given to the gift of knowing the pitch of any sounded note. The lack of a talent which did not have any real connection with general musical sense but which my mother possessed entirely, gave me no peace. If music had been my profession, as seemed the case to an outsider, I would not have been interested in this absolute pitch, I knew that outstanding contemporary composers did not possess it, and that it is thought Wagner and Tchaikovsky did not command it. But for me music was a cult, that is it was that ruinous point to which everything which was most superstitious and self-denying in me gathered, and because of this, each time that my will grew wings on an evening's inspiration, I hastened to humble it in the morning, reminding myself again of my so-called defect.

All the same I had several serious works. Now I was to show them to my idol. I set about making arrangements for a meeting, one so natural in view of the friendship of our respective homes, with a characteristic excess of effort. This step, one which would have seemed importunate to me in any circumstances, grew before my eyes into a kind of sacrilege in actual fact. And on the appointed day, making my way to Glazovsky, where Scriabin was living for the time being, I was taking him not so much my compositions but a love which had long outgrown expression and my apologies for my imagined lack of tact to which I admitted I had been led unwillingly. The crowded number 4 squeezed and jolted these emotions, bearing them mercilessly to the terrifyingly approaching goal along the brown Arbat which was being dragged to the Smolensky by shaggy and sweaty cows, horses and pedestrians, knee-deep in water.

IV

I appreciated then how well trained are our facial muscles. Unable to breathe properly from nervousness I mumbled something with a dry tongue and washed down my replies with frequent swallows of tea so as not to choke or make matters worse in some other way.

The skin began to creep along my jaw-bones and the protuberances of my forehead, I moved my eyebrows, nodded and smiled, and each time I touched the creases of this mimicry upon the bridge of my nose, creases ticklish and sticky like cobwebs, I discovered my handkerchief clutched convulsively in my hand and with it again and again I wiped the large beads of sweat from my brow. Behind my head, spring, bound by the curtains, rose smokily over the whole mews. In front, between my hosts who were trying with redoubled talkativeness to guide me out of my difficulties, the tea exhaled in the cups, the samovar hissed pierced by its arrow of steam, and the sun, misted with water and manure, circled upwards. The smoke of a stump of cigar, wavy like a tortoiseshell comb, pulled its way from the ashtray to the light, on reaching which it crawled repletely along it sideways as though it were a piece of felt. I don't know why, but this circling of blinded air, the steaming waffles, smoking sugar and silver burning like paper, heightened my nervousness unbearably. It subsided when going across to the salon I found myself at the piano.

I was still nervous when I played the first piece, when I came to the second I had almost recovered my control, during the third I surrendered myself to the pressure of the new and unforeseen. Accidentally my gaze fell on the listener.

Following the progress of the performance, first he raised his head, then his brows, finally all flushed, he got up himself and accompanying the variations of the melody with the elusive variations of his smile, glided towards me on its rhythmic perspective. He liked all this. I hastened to finish. Immediately he began assuring me that it was clumsy to speak of talent for music when something incomparably bigger was on hand and it was open to me to say my word in music. Referring to the phrases which had flashed by he sat down to the piano, to repeat one which had particularly attracted him. The harmony was complicated and I did not expect him to reproduce it exactly, but another unexpected thing happened, he repeated it in the wrong key, and the flaw which had tormented me all these years splashed from under his fingers as his own.

And again preferring the eloquence of fact to the instability of guesswork, I trembled and started thinking along two lines of thought. If he would admit to me: "Borya, why even I have not got it," then it would be all right, then, it would mean that I was not binding myself to music, but that music itself was my fate. But if in answer the conversation turned on Wagner, Tchaikovsky, on piano-tuners and so forth – but I was already approaching the nerve-racking subject, and interrupted in the middle of a word was already swallowing in reply. "Absolute pitch? After everything I have said to you? And what of Wagner? And Tchaikovsky? And hundreds of piano-tuners who have it?"

We were walking up and down the room. He would put his hand on my shoulder or take my arm. He talked of the harm of improvising, about when, why and how one should compose. For examples of simplicity to which one should always aspire, he instanced his own sonatas, notorious for their complexity. He took his examples of culpable complexity from the most banal literatures of the romances. The paradox of his comparisons did not worry me. I agreed that formlessness is more complex than form. That an unguarded volubility seems attainable because it is empty. That spoilt by the emptiness of trite patterns we take just that exceptional copiousness coming after long desuetude for the mannerisms of form. Imperceptibly he came to more definite advice. He questioned me about my education and, learning that I had chosen the faculty of law on account of its simplicity, advised me to change without delay to the philosophical section of the historico-philological, which I duly did on the following day. And while he talked I thought over what had happened. I did not break my arrangement with fate, but I remembered the bad issue of my guess. Did this incident dethrone my god? No, never – it lifted him from his former height to yet another. Why did he deny me that most straightforward reply for which I so longed? That was his secret. At some time when it would be already too late, he would bestow upon me this omitted confession. How had he allayed his own youthful doubts? That too was his secret and it was this which raised him to a new height. However, it was long dark in the room, the lamps were alight in the mews, it was time to know when to go.

I did not know, as I took my leave, how to thank him. Something welled up in me. Something tore and sought for freedom. Something wept and something exulted.

The very first rush of cool street air told of houses and distances. Their uproar rose skywards, wafted off the cobblestones in the general harmony of a Moscow night. I remembered my parents impatiently preparing their questions. However I might make my statement it would bear no interpretation except the very happiest. And it was only at this point that submitting to the logic of the forthcoming recital I faced the fortunate events of the day as a fact. They did not belong to me in such a guise. As accomplished facts they became matters auguring a future outcome only for others. However much the news I was carrying to my people might excite me, I did not feel calm at heart. But much more like happiness was my admission that just this sadness could not be poured into anyone's ears, and that like my future, it would be left there below, down in the street, there with my Moscow, mine in this hour as never before. I walked along the side streets and crossed the road more often than was necessary. Absolutely without my being conscious of it, the world which only the day before had seemed innate in me forever, was melting and breaking up inside me. I walked along gathering speed at every corner and I did not know that that night I was already breaking with music.

Greece distinguished herself excellently among the ages. She understood how to meditate on childhood, which is as sealed up and independent as an initial integrated kernel. How greatly she possessed this talent, can be seen in her myth of Ganymede and many others that are similar. The same convictions entered her interpretations of the demigod and the hero. In her opinion, some portion of risk and tragedy must be gathered sufficiently early in a handful, which can be gazed upon and understood in a flash. Certain sections of the edifice, and among these the principal arch of fatalism, must be laid once and for all from the very outset in the interests of its future proportions. And finally, death itself must be experienced, possibly in some memorable similitude.

And this is why the ancients, with an art that was generalized, ever unexpected, enthralling as a fairy-tale, still knew nothing of Romanticism.

Brought up on a demand never afterwards made on anyone, on a superworld of deeds and problems, she was completely ignorant of the superworld as a personal effect. She was ensured against that because she prescribed for childhood the whole dose of the extraordinary that is to be found in the world. And according to her ways, when man entered gigantic reality with gigantic steps, both his coming out and his surroundings were accounted ordinary.

First published in Russian: 1931
Translation by Robert Payne

Дух Музыки
Борис Поплавский

Над балом музыки сияли облака,
Горела зелень яркая у входа,
Там жизнь была, а в десяти шагах
Синела ночь и плыли в вечность годы.
Мы танцевали нашу жизнь под шум
Огромных труб, где рокотало время,
Смеялся пьяный видя столько лун
Уснувших в розах и объятых тленьем.
На зовы труб, над пропастью авгурной,
С крылами ярких флагов на плечах,
Прошли танцоры поступью бравурной,
Как блеск ракет блуждающих в ночах.
Они смеялись, плакали, грустили.
Бросали розы к отраженьям звезд,
Таинственные книги возносили,
Вдали смолкали перейдя за мост.
Все исчезало, гасло, обрывалось,
А музыка кричала "Хор вперед",
Ломала руки в переулке жалость
И музыку убить звала народ.
Но ангелы играли безмятежно.
Их слушали: трава, цветы и дети,
Кружась, танцоры целовались нежно
И просыпались на другой планете.
Казалось им они цвели в аду,
А далеко внизу был воздух синий.
Дух музыки мечтал в ночном саду
С энигматической улыбкой соловьиной.
Там бал погас. Там был рассвет, покой
Лишь тонкою железною рукой
Наигрывала смерть за упокой
Вставало тихо солнце за рекой.

Spirit of Music
Boris Poplavsky

Above the music's ball clouds glowed and flared,
and greenery burned brightly at the door –
one sensed life's presence, while ten steps away
night blued, and years flowed off forevermore.
We danced our life to the tremendous sounds
of massive trumpets – where time thundered out,
a drunk laughed when he saw so many moons
asleep in roses and embraced by rot.
Summoned by trumpets, over augury's abyss,
shoulders adorned with wings of dazzling flags,
the dancers whirled at a bravura pace,
like glaring rockets wandering the nights.
They laughed, they cried, and they grew melancholy,
they tossed their roses to the stars' reflections,
raised to the heavens their mysterious volumes,
fell quiet past the bridge, far in the distance.
And all was breaking off, and vanishing, and fading –
music alone was shouting "Chorus, forward!"
while pity wrung its hands in some dark alley,
urging the masses to kill music off.
And yet the angels played on undisturbed.
The grass, the flowers, and the children heard it.
Dancers kissed tenderly, while whirling on and on,
and then awoke upon another planet.
Although the air was blue far down below them,
they felt that they were blossoming in hell.
Music's own spirit dreamt in a night garden,
wearing a nightingale's most enigmatic smile.
The ball burned out. And there was dawn, and peace.
And death alone strummed with its spindly fingers
of iron for the soul's eternal rest.
The sun rose quietly beyond the river.

First published in Russian: 1930
Translation by Boris Dralyuk

Песенка короткая, как жизнь сама
Булат Окуджава

Песенка короткая, как жизнь сама,
Где-то в дороге услышанная.
У неё пронзительные слова,
А мелодия почти что возвышенная.

Она появляется с рассветом вдруг,
Медлить и врать не обученная,
Она,как надежда из первых рук,
В дар от природы полученная.

От двери к дверям,из окна в окно,
В след за тобой она тянется,
Всё умрет,чему суждено,
Только она останется.

Песенка короткая,как жизнь сама,
Где-то в дороге услышанная.
У неё пронзительные слова,
А мелодия почти что возвышенная.

Song Short as Life
Bulat Okudzhava

Song you might hear somewhere while on a stroll,
Song short as life, so soon halted,
Song with brave words that pierce into your soul
And melody close to exalted.

It comes all at once at the first break of dawn,
Without a false note, nothing missing,
Giving you hope you had thought all but gone –
It's a gift straight from nature, a blessing.

Since then in your life this song will remain.
Wherever you go it will find you.
All things must die, that is ordained,
But this song will live on behind you.

Song you might hear somewhere while on a stroll,
Song short as life, so soon halted,
Song with brave words that pierce into your soul
And melody close to exalted.

First published in Russian: 1984
Translation by Lydia Razran Stone
with Vladimir Kovner

Babel's "The Song" comes from his *Red Cavalry* cycle, a volume of short stories about the Polish-Soviet War (1919-1921). As in many of these pieces, Babel contrasts the narrator's intellectual, poetic outlook with the brutalities and horrors of war.

The Song
Isaac Babel

When we were quartered in the village of Budziatycze, it was my lot to end up with an evil landlady. She was a widow, she was poor. I broke many locks on her storerooms, but found no provisions.

All I could do was to try and outsmart her, and one fine day, coming home early before dusk, I caught her closing the door of the stove, which was still warm. The hut smelled of cabbage soup, and there might well have been some meat in that soup. I did smell meat in her soup and laid my revolver on the table, but the old woman denied everything. Her face and black fingers were gripped by spasms, she glowered at me with fear and extraordinary hatred. Nothing would have saved her – I would have made her own up with my revolver if Sashka Konyayev, in other words Sashka Christ, hadn't suddenly turned up.

He came into the hut with his concertina under his arm, his exquisite legs shuffling in battered boots.

"How about a song?" Sashka said, looking at me, his eyes filled with blue and dreamy ice crystals. "How about a song?" he said, and sat down on the bench and played a prelude.

The pensive prelude came as if from far away. He stopped, and his blue eyes filled with longing. He turned away, and, knowing what I liked, started off on a song from Kuban.

"Star of the fields," he sang, "star of the fields over my native hut, and my mother's hand, so sorrowful...."

I loved that song. Sashka knew this, because both of us, both he and I, had first heard this song back in '19 in the shallows of the Don in the Cossack village of Kagalnitskaya.

A hunter who poached in the protected waters there had taught it to us. There, in the protected waters, fish spawn and countless flocks of birds nest. The fish multiply in the shallows in incredible numbers, you can scoop them up with a ladle or even with your bare hands, and if you dip your oar in the water, it just stands there upright – a fish will have grabbed it and will carry it away. We saw this with our own eyes, we will never forget the protected waters of Kagalnitskaya. Every government has banned hunting there – a good ban – but back in '19 a war was raging in the shallows, and Yakov the hunter, who plied his forbidden trade right before our eyes, gave Sashka Christ, our squadron singer, a concertina as a present so that we would look the other way. He taught Sashka his songs. Many of them were soulful, old songs. So we forgave the roguish hunter, for we needed his songs: back then, no one could see the war ever ending, and Sashka covered our arduous paths with melody and tears. A bloody trail followed our paths. The songs soared over this trail. That is how it was in Kuban and on our campaigns against the Greens,[1] and that is how it was in the Urals and in the Caucasian foothills, and that is how it is to this very day. We need

1. Defectors from the Imperial army and later also from the new Soviet army, who banded together in guerrilla groups. They were called "Greens" because they hid in forests. Both the Whites and the Reds tried to organize them under their influence, creating bands of Red Greens and White Greens.

these songs, no one can see this war ever ending, and Sashka Christ, our squadron singer, is too young to die.

And this evening too, cheated of my landlady's cabbage soup, Sashka calmed me with his soft, wavering voice.

"Star of the fields," he sang, "star of the fields over my native hut, and my mother's hand, so sorrowful…"

And I listened, stretched out in a corner on my rotting bedding. A dream broke my bones, the dream shook the putrid hay beneath me, and through the dream's burning torrent I could barely make out the old woman, who was standing by the wall, her withered cheek propped on her hand. She hung her ravaged head and stood fixed by the wall, not moving even after Sashka had finished playing. Sashka finished and put down his concertina, yawned, and burst out laughing as after a long sleep, and then, noticing the chaos in the widow's hut, he wiped the debris from the bench and brought in a bucket of water.

"You see, deary, what your boss is up to?" the landlady said to him, pointing at me and rubbing her back against the door. "Your boss came in here, yelled at me, stamped his foot, broke all the locks in my house, and shoved his gun at me. It is a sin before the Lord to shove a gun at me – I'm a woman, after all!"

She rubbed her back against the door again and threw a sheepskin coat over her son. Her son lay snoring beneath an icon on a large bed covered with rags. He was a deaf-mute boy with a white, water-swollen head and gigantic feet, like those of a grown *muzhik*. His mother wiped the snot from his nose and came back to the table.

"Mistress," Sashka said to her, caressing her shoulder, "if you wish, I could be really nice to you."

But it was as if the woman hadn't heard what he had said.

"I didn't see no cabbage soup at all," she said, her cheek propped on her hand. "It ran away, my cabbage soup, and people shove their guns at me, so that even when a nice man comes along and I get a chance to tumble a little, I've ended up feeling so drab, I can't even enjoy sinning!"

She dragged out her mournful lament and, mumbling, rolled her deaf-mute son to the wall. Sashka lay with her on the rag-covered bed while I tried to sleep, conjuring up dreams so that I would doze off with pleasant thoughts.

First published in Russian: 1926
Translation by Peter Constantine

Сияла ночь
Афанасий Фет

Сияла ночь. Луной был полон сад. Лежали
Лучи у наших ног в гостиной без огней.
Рояль был весь раскрыт, и струны в нем дрожали,
Как и сердца у нас за песнию твоей.
Ты пела до зари, в слезах изнемогая,
Что ты одна – любовь, что нет любви иной,
И так хотелось жить, чтоб, звука не роняя,
Тебя любить, обнять и плакать над тобой.
И много лет прошло, томительных и скучных,
И вот в тиши ночной твой голос слышу вновь,
И веет, как тогда, во вздохах этих звучных,
Что ты одна – вся жизнь, что ты одна – любовь.
Что нет обид судьбы и сердца жгучей муки,
А жизни нет конца, и цели нет иной,
Как только веровать в рыдающие звуки,
Тебя любить, обнять и плакать над тобой!

Silver Night
Afanasy Fet

A silver night. The moon suffused the park. Cascading
Rays on the parlor floor, the only light that shone.
The piano open wide, strings trembling, resonating,
Just like our hearts, as you sang love songs all your own.
You sang until it dawned, your voice in sweet tears breaking,
That you embodied love, and love meant only you.
And I so wished to live: all other songs forsaking,
To love you, hold you close, and shed tears over you.
Now many years have passed, profoundly dull and onerous,
Then in the still of night I hear your voice anew,
Just as in days gone by, in sighs so sweetly sonorous,
That you embody life, and love means only you,
There is no cruel fate, no pangs of heartache burning,
There is no end to life, no other aim so true
As simply to have faith in these lost sounds of yearning,
To love you, hold you close, and shed tears over you!

First published in Russian: 1877
Translation by Lawrence Bogoslaw
with Lydia Razran Stone

STATEMENT OF OWNERSHIP, MANAGEMENT AND CIRCULATION. Title: Russian Life. **Publication number:** 1939-7240. **Frequency:** Quarterly. **Issues per year:** 4. **Annual Subscription price:** $35. **Mailing address:** PO Box 567, Montpelier, VT 05601-0567. **Phone:** 802-223-4955. **Publisher:** Paul E. Richardson. **Editor:** Olga Kuzmina (both at address above). **Owner:** Russian Information Services, Inc. **Circulation statistics** (July 1, 2015 issue; figures in parentheses are average for the preceding 12 months). **Total number of copies:** 500 (486). **Paid and/or requested circulation:** 401 (427). **Free distribution by mail:** 19 (32). **Free distribution outside the mail:** 50 (12). **Total free distribution:** 69 (44). **Total distribution:** 470 (471). **Copies not distributed:** 30 (15). **Total:** 500 (486). **Percent paid and/or requested circulation:** 85.32% (90.69%). Filed with the USPS on October 1, 2015. Paul Richardson, Publisher.

Made in the USA
Charleston, SC
25 September 2015